THE HORNSWOGGLE
FLIM-FLAM

The Hornswoggle Flim-Flam

A CLASS '94 MYSTERY

ARIA CREEK

IANOM

First Printing, 2024

For Elizabeth and Nicole Bowman

&

all my readers who go wandering into my world
of "Shiny" female protagonists

Also by Aria Creek

The Class'94 Mystery Series
The Exchange
The Letter
The Hornswoggle Flim-Flam

The LI'MA series
I Think Therefore I Am
Cascade

Prime Hollingsworth-Suazo
Vengence

Siddhartha, The Brahim's Daughter

The Eight Members of Class '94

Our Three Champion Cyclists

Casey Buckhauser

Susan Lively-Hill

Whitney House

Our Tennis Champion

Samanthea Robinson

Our Downhill Medalist

Char'elene Johansen

Our Three Softball Champions

Amel'iya Jackson

Grace Philamore Montgomery

Claire Elizabeth Stockton

1

I lay motionless; blissfully enjoying the sweet sensation of my sleep drenched body calmly floating its way up to full wakefulness; leaving the past snugly tucked away ... out of sight ... and out of mind.

(HA! Tucked away! Maybe. But ... maybe the corners weren't tight enough.)

Through my bedroom window, a sliver of dawn light was breaking into the surrounding darkness, heralding the second day of the bacchanal called Spring break. A time where mostly college age humans go berserk in mind and body; doing the most foolish naïve things that they will ever do in their entire lives.

(When I was their age, Spring Break was something quite foreign to me and my friends. I don't think Class '94 knew what youthful exuberance was back then. But that's the past.)

At the moment, there were nine kids I knew who were on the loose in this conflagration of excess and youthful exuberance.

Today, all of those nine children that encircle the constellation named Class '94, are at home or have run away to parts I don't want to know about. All of them are my godchildren, and I like them ... but ... they're all high maintenance. Frankly, I like unencumberment (the state of being blissfully unencumbered).

So ... there I lay, in my elegant bedroom; an original Class '94 Sam & Grace creation. (Grace, a champion baseball player in high school, is our clothing experts and Sam, a professional tennis medal winner, is our home decor designer.)

Within the four walls of my unencumbered room exists one wildly extravagant (one of a kind, I am told) bed, a few windows and a door.

The bare walls are painted bright robin's egg sky blue.

The windows have drapes, that billow at the floor and are pulled back with ties. (Sam insisted. I fought. I lost. They've grown on me.) Drapes which I almost never close.

Now, the best part is the bed. Great firm foam mattress covered in sheets which are as soft as a floating summer cloud. Yummy. And a luscious floral printed duvet covered the bed and me. (The design is a Class '94's Whitney textile design original. Whitney's our champion cyclist turned famous artist.)

The cover is filled with the softest, lightest down … ethically sourced of course. (There was a time when ethically sourced and organic were not in the vocabulary of the poor girl I used to be.)

Well, I'm not poor anymore and I'm determined to stay that way so I took a deep breath, absorbing the last silent ephemeral sliver of predawn light and up I got to begin my day.

In under eight minutes, I did the bathroom thing, put on my high-end running gear, made my way downstairs, grabbed my water bottle and was on my way out to the garage.

I swung my leg over my 350 cc classic orange trimmed motorcycle (which was not too small, not too big, and just the right size for zipping over to the high school. Yeash! OK! So it's a Ducati). I turned on the headlights (so no half-asleep early-worker drove over me) and headed out to meet Sam at the high school track.

It's been more than two decades since the eight of us, all high school champion athletes, christened ourselves Class'94.

Besides the medals, accolades and fans going berserk whenever each one of us won a tournament, there are perks to being Kerry high school's very successful athletic champions. For instance: we each have a key for the locked gate that surrounded the school's regulation sized track. The track where Sam and I run three times a week (when we're both in town).

Besides the use of their six-lane track there's also the tennis courts. Sam, our high school tennis champion who turned professional, takes advantage of these courts. Her tall well-proportioned mesomorph body needs to run and do the courts to keep her from turning into a blob.

Me? I'm slim, tall, broad shouldered and just love to run. That's how I got my education. I ran for scholarships, the Elvira Fitzpatrick way.

Our beneficent angel of a high school coach made sure all eight of us were the best at the sport she chose for each of us. She drilled and molded us into champions, and scholarship worthy material.

And champions we became and scholarships we won.

All eight of us.

Casey, my next door neighbor, having the athlete's body configuration similar to mine, became a champion cyclist (riding for scholarship money throughout college, with Whitney and Susan. The three of them became known as the trinity on wheels).

In high school, Grace played baseball with me and Amel'iya (the unmentionable eighth one (I'll get to that later; maybe). Grace skipped the square on the board that read college, she stayed in Kerry, starting the best clothing store for hundreds of miles … in all directions. (This is her PR. But it's based on truth and testimonials.)

Of all eight of us, Char'Elene, is our need-for-speed demon. Skiing is her forte. A lot of downhill wins and an Olympic medal gave her the money to become a doctor.

Poor we may have all been, but not anymore. (With poverty came it's evil twin, dysfunctional families, abuse and hopelessness; but, that's all so behind us now. Absolutely. Positively.)

2

Sam and I did our run and an hour later I was back home.

A two story renovated brick house, topped with a mansard roof and four little windows peeking out. There's a small garden out front and a larger one in back. Both are tended to by invisible professional gnomes. Magic people who know how to keep things that grow from dying. This is very important if you have a garden.

(Even though they're absolutely invisible (I've never seen them) I know they've been here because 1) the gardens are always picture perfect 2) I get a bill.)

I pulled into my one-car garage which had just enough room for my hybrid car and the cycle.

I locked up and ran into the house. I was on a tight schedule this morning.

I took a fast shower, grabbed an outfit out of the closet and raced downstairs in time for my early morning zoom call to New York.

I'm a tech wiz, both hardware and software, even have patents to prove it, and I had anxious clients in New York that needed to talk.

I was wearing one of the casual work outfits (that's what Grace calls them - she's our clothes wizard as I've mentioned) that make me look good on a zoom call. (Grace actually did a test. She forced me to try on way too many outfits until she found the ones to her satisfaction. Outfits that didn't make me fade away or buzz on screen. She would know what works and what doesn't ... she owns (with Sam) what really is the best clothing/home décor store east of the Mississippi and west of the Hudson River.)

I call the color of the long sleeve t-shirt I was wearing, mustard. Grace calls it something fancy that I refuse to remember. I wore it with a pair of really nice deep purple pants (the color has a fancy name too, and yes, I refuse to remember that also).

And so my day started.

3

I'm Claire Elizabeth Stockton. I'm one of seven women (used to be eight - I'm referring to the unmentionable Amel'iya) who are known throughout the kingdom as The Class of '94.

You can consider us a click, a pod, a troop, a cauldron, or in plain English an exceptional group of champion athletes - way back in high school - who continued on throughout our college years (except for Grace as I mentioned. She went into business).

We formed a tight knit bond back in those hard days. A bond that's held us together through the muck and mire of life ... so far (sometimes by the slimmest of threads).

(Except for the one that betrayed us. She, the unmentionable, as I've mentioned, the one we don't talk about.)

We hail from Kerry, Ohio. (A small, now gentrified town within driving distance of metropolises like Cleveland and Columbus.)

The seven of us (even the missing one) came from that part of town where poor black, poor brown and a lot of white-trash mixed but never matched. It was a place that was dangerous and tough for all the kids.

(I will note here, that we've all moved on from our depressing, mostly dysfunctional beginnings. Letting you know this up front, because we'd rather you cheer us than feel sorry for us.)

Besides the bad streets where we grew up, there was another part of town marked off for the struggling but not considered poor whites, while another small part was for prosperous blacks, and another practically gigantic part for prosperous whites. It was like a bunch of gangs or thugs marking off their territories with invisible electrified twenty foot high fencing.

Today, I live in a beautiful house next door to my closest friend Casey Buckhauser (in one of the run-down, but now gentrified, tree lined parts of town).

Casey, (who is the second in command of our group) and her husband Mitch have three children. I call them the Wild Bunch. They are the reason people should think twice before having children.

At the moment, their daughter was banging on my front door. Yes I have a doorbell. No she wasn't using it.

I watched her on my security screen as I was ending my business call to the client in New York, which would necessitate worming my way through their system after they closed for the day, hunting down whatever smash-up their internal tech person did.

I do a lot of this kind of clean up. When it's a smash-up on a program I delicately hand wove for them I get really testy with my client. Which was the mood I was in right now.

Casey's daughter had given up knocking and had now moved on to ringing my doorbell like a normal person.

I hung up on my client, looked over at the screen again which showed her looking up into the security camera while her finger kept pressing the bell. I need to rig something to stop the bell from ringing at moments like this.

She appeared determined. She wasn't giving up. So, I had to let her in.

4

Casey's daughter Mia, came charging into my house wearing stove-pipe jeans I'd swear she'd painted onto her body, and a long-sleeve tank top that might have been painted on too. A studded belt was around her waist and a pair of ankle boots with a wedge heel were on her feet. All new stuff.

She had a growth spurt this year that put her eye to eye with her mom and into the next clothing size. That's why all the new threads.

Today, Mia, a tall willowy reed of a teenager, was a young woman dressed for battle.

This week her hair was short, with a sharp wedge cut out on the side that looked stunning, and, happened to match the wedge boots on her feet. I think it was done on purpose.

Sometimes she wears her hair long, sometimes short, sometimes straightened, sometimes natural and sometimes in rows. The only thing she hasn't tried yet is bald.

She's Casey's middle child and one of my many, like way too many godchildren.

I closed the door behind her as she blew past me.

After closing the door, I followed in her wake through my entrance hallway.

A hallway where a small break-away kitchen was to my left and a half bathroom was to my right. These small but necessary rooms were inconsequential because they were swallowed up and practically disappeared due to the enormity of the room that Sam (of the aforementioned early morning track run partner) one of my eight (now seven, ugh) terrific Class'94 friends, had created out of three rooms on the first floor of my house.

Samanthea had re-designed, demolished and re-built my living room, slash office, slash workspace as her first Interior Design project when she and Grace expanded their retail fashion business into home and office Interiors and decor.

The space that Sam created for me is brilliant, if I must say so myself. The floors are stained a deep gray, almost black, accented by the light wood used for all the built-in's. Like desks, cubby holes, drawers, shelves.

She achieved the effect of making the whole room look like it was floating in the air. It had the "Wow" effect that impressed those clients who came in person.

She also used the light wood for framing the entire wall that was glass windows and doors. The glorious view past this wide expanse of light and sky was of my landscaped and brick walled garden. (Attended to by the aforementioned magical gnomes.)

Casey calls it my retreat from the maddening world.

I don't really need the upscale interior layout, but Sam and Grace think I do ... and they always win when it comes to clothes and home/ office decor.

The open floorplan is amazingly comfortable, has lots of breathing room and enough hidey-holes to store the accessories which I need to build, repair or invent tech stuff.

In case I didn't mention it, not only am I a tech genius but I own my own business - which is why I was within arm's reach of Mia the day that she wanted to be filled in on all the blanks in her mom's history ... therefore her own history.

Mia was now sitting in one of my many comfortable client chairs.

After giving me an extensive buildup and rationale for wanting the historical information she was asking me to provide, Mia demanded, "Aunt Claire you have to tell me what happened."

I'd listened patiently. Then I said, "Go ask your mother?" This is my standard answer to all my godchildren's questions.

"She just brushes me off! And the Reverend Cooper is coming soon, and I just have to know!" she wined.

I hate when she wines; so I gave her my-get-out-of-here look to which she immediately composed herself. Why Casey can't do this with any of her kids I don't know. It seems easy enough to me.

"If your mother doesn't want to tell you then …"

"It's not that she doesn't want to tell me," she interrupted, "it's that she doesn't think it's important or relevant or whatever. But I think she did something cool and saved the Reverend from something terrible. For god's sake Aunt Claire, Matie Cooper's my great aunt and I don't know their history. Well not all of it anyway. Not the juicy parts."

I looked at her and sat back in my very comfortable CEO chair. A chair that Samanthea Robinson, had replaced three or four times already. She insists that the chair be kept fresh, firm, comfortable and up to date, especially since I spend so much of my time in it. And since she is the decorator extraordinaire of Class'94 I go along with it.

And even if I didn't go along … she'd switch the chairs out anyway. I don't argue anymore with Sam or her partner in fashion Grace Philamore Montgomery, because they always win and they're always right.

So, there I sat deciding what to say. Since I couldn't make up my mind I did the only sensible thing I could think of.

I called Casey.

Mia cringed, putting on one of her hopeless defeated faces. I ignored her which of course made her go into exasperation mode.

As I waited for Casey to answer her phone, I just smiled at Mia. She started to moan and groan.

I said a few words to Casey and ended the call.

"So what did mom say?" Mia said, despondently expecting the worst.

"She said yes."

"Just yes? No if ands or buts?"

"Just yes," I assured her to which I was given the broadest smile the child could muster.

"So?" she pushed.

"So, don't call me Aunt Claire – I'm not your aunt," I said, making it a condition for my cooperation. I hate the teenage whining and being called aunt.

She pursed her lips, scrunched up her face and said in her most imperious voice, "OK … godmother Stockton … please tell me about my mom and her aunt."

I took a deep breath, tried not to laugh and began, "It was back during the crazy months before the clock turned over to January 1, 2000.

It was a time when everyone thought the world would collapse, disintegrate or unravel.

It was a time when the specter of the Y2K bug was suspended over the world like an acid breathing evil monster ready to suck-out all the 1's and 0's in a vampire feast.

It was a time where the chains, locks and firewalls of "Cyber Security" was nowhere near robust as is it today.

The turn of the millennium was a time when people thought planes would crash, trains would career off their tracks, bank vaults wouldn't open, communication links would melt down, rockets would go off and Armageddon would be upon us.

Into this fevered madhouse came the Preacher.

5

Preacher Charmeur arrived in Gening, New York in the early spring; at the same time the first tulips of the season burst upon the scene in all their glory.

At first glance he appeared to have just walked off a movie set, like he was in costume... some would say. Rather ordinary in appearance ... others would say. Enigmatic charismatic and riveting ... most would agree.

The preacher was a tall man. Scrawny and bow legged. His black hair was shaved close to the scalp, his dark eyes were deep set under bushy eyebrows.

His long nose, manicured mustache and firm bony chin, all jutted out in front of him as he walked, like he was daring anyone to take a fist to that part of his anatomy.

What gave the impression of his walking off a movie set, well, besides the exaggerated tall wide brimmed black hat and old western gunslinger movie mustache, were his clothes.

He wore a combination of clerical stiffness and dangerous goth, with large laced shoes that were spit polish shinned.

His outfit was neither proper Catholic, Protestant, Baptist or even Evangelical. What it was ... was noticeable.

His appearance was only second to the combination of power and humility that emanated like perfume from the man, which was strikingly contagious but not unusual for a religious-performer.

Within a week of his arrival, in a late model four door Chrysler, he took up residence in a second-floor apartment, that was neither lavish nor rundown. It was just one of the many ordinary apartments available in Gening at that time.

The Main Street corner apartment may have been innocuous and bland but it did have what the preacher needed. It had a convenient back door, a main entrance on the side street, plus he was able to quietly arrange access to the fledgling internet.

At that time the internet resembled the wild west of tech wizardry where a hacker could use "capabilities" existing in algorithms, software and programs, at will. (Plus the availability was sketchy outside of big cities.)

It could easily be said of the preacher that he looked like a man who had come to town to settle down and do good works.

But the Reverend Dr. Matie Cooper of the Springrock Baptist Church knew otherwise. She couldn't explain it. But something was definitely off.

The new preacher man didn't quite hit the mark.

6

The earth didn't shake rattle or roll, explode, erupt or fall down, just because Charmeur came to town.

Time passed. Spring turned into summer and drifted slowly into autumn where the air was crisp with a warm stroke as it gently drifted through the open windows of the small vestry attached to the Springrock Baptist church where Reverend Dr. Matie Cooper had led the congregation for the past twenty some odd years.

The church was a tall impressive edifice, with its tall bell tower and a pair of solid wooden doors out front. Being that the building came right up to the sidewalk out front, there wasn't any room for a bench, a bush or a flower.

The old church, located on a quiet residential street was flanked on both sides by houses that had small front yards, most with flowers and some with trimmed hedges softening the austerity of the church in its midst. Each of the houses on both sides of the street had a wide drive-way which added to the uncluttered friendly look of the area.

Off to the right side of the church was the vestry. A simple square room with flowered wallpaper that Matie had installed herself. She was partial to bluebells, which exploded over every unused wall space.

The furthest side of the room, from the door that lead into the church, held a writing desk that Matie had found at a yard sale, a deep-seated desk chair and two sturdy comfortable unholstered chairs, in front of her desk.

The things that Matie loved the most about her office, were the two curtained windows flanking either side of her desk. (Each one had a small beautifully cut stained-glass panel set atop the long rectangle window below it.)

Both windows now stood open.

Underneath each window stood four short wooden filing cabinets, standing side by side. Matie had placed mementoes and gifts that she'd been given or acquired over the years on top of the cabinets.

And then there were the shelves. Lots of them. Covering two walls, from floor to ceiling, with a ladder to reach the top most shelves. Between services, the bibles were collected and safely stored on three of these shelves.

The wall, opposite the Reverend's desk, had three doors, and watercolors on whatever wall space was available. One of the doors was for a large closet. Another one for a small bathroom with a changing area. The third lead into the church.

The watercolors were painted by Whitney (Class '94's resident artist) that were beautifully framed and mounted on the wall.

Matie's pocketbook could only stretch to watercolors. Her choices of what to buy, showed her keen eye for the best that Whitney had to offer. (Whenever Whitney had a show in New York City, Matie made it a point to get onto the Metro North train going south in order to see it.)

The warm breeze floating on the evening air was gently filling the room with scents from the neighbors garden. In the comfortable and welcoming atmosphere of the rearranged vestry sat the Reverend and her small evening group.

In the center of the room, stood a folding table covered with a plain lavender tablecloth. It held a large plate of ginger snap cookies and a tall pitcher of lemonade with glasses.

The group attending this evening's discussion, consisted of six women, ages 72 to 26. They all found the two hours they spent on Tuesday nights - exciting.

The Reverend would joke that her congregants attended these Tuesday meetings - partly because of the unusual subject matter - partly because of the humor she insinuated surreptitiously into the conversation and partly because she made the best ginger snap cookies east of the Hudson River.

7

The subject under discussion this evening was a bit unusual; especially to the conservative old timers in the congregation. But they never attended. Mostly they did a lot of eye rolling and humphfing.

A number of the progressive open-minded women in her congregation, had requested a series of discussions on whether or not women have any real power in religion, home and the community.

When Matie first announced the start of this particular group discussion there was a minor earthquake felt in Gening.

Mostly out of fear.

Some objected.

Power and women were not used in the same sentence or worlds that some of Matie's congregants lived in.

But the women who had signed up for this particular group responded, "For goodness sake we have a fine intelligent reverend woman at our pulpit and she speaks to the truth." It took a little smoothing of feathers and a lot of one on one conversations where Matie listened to all the protests, but in the end the women in the group prevailed.

Still, this was not San Francisco. Generally speaking, Matie's congregants were neither hippie, heavy metal nor new age. They were basically a conservative flock with a strong thin streak of liberal morals; all ensconced in a traditionally housed solid century-old brick and mortar Church which had a grand high steeple and a tall stained-glass windows that bespoke of its long life in this part of the Hudson Valley in upstate New York.

The upper Hudson River Valley basin had been home to the likes of Woodhull, the first female presidential candidate (before women could vote) and the Woman suffragette movement, whose ideas and progeny still have their roots deeply embedded in the soil.

Back then, granting women the right to vote, was considered a white woman's issue. Black women were not included in the country wide organizations that sprang up around the suffragette movement; but black women fought and marched anyway. But, as the Reverend had discussed with the group, these women are mostly still hidden by history.

The Reverend had made it a point to tell her women's group that not only did these black women march for the right of black women to vote, but also for women's equality at a time when very few women, of any denomination or race, put voting and equality together.

The history of tough, forward thinking and brilliant women in the region, who fought for their right to vote, and then for equality, was one of the reasons Matie chose this eastern state to settle down in.

And here she was, starting the sixth group session, in this series, on a balmy night in the Hudson Valley.

The Reverend Dr. Matie Cooper looked around at her eager group of women and began in the cadence of her firm resonating bible preaching voice:

IN the beginning ... Way back in time – way before read'in and writ'in – the concept of god took on many images and many forms.

During this time ...

    ONE man created a god.
        Created a god in his Own image.
Then ...

ONE, sweet ...
kind woman ...
LOOKED upon this man ...
and she
PITIED

> *him.*
> *YES! I say,*
> *pitied him.*

> > *Silently.*

Throughout the thousands of Centuries to follow,
> *MORE men came along*
> > *and they ALSO*

> > > *created their own gods,*
> > > *in their OWN image.*

Women of those times,
> *looked upon those men,*
> *and as from time immemorial,*

> > *They PITIED the men*
> > > *Silently.*

All these women,
> *these smart, kind women ... THEY knew ...*

> > *Yes THEY knew ...*
> > *they knew a SECRET*

> *...*

They knew that spirituality
> *is the FOUNDATION*
Yes, I say the very foundation
> *which belief is based upon.*

The kind of SPIRITUALITY

Yes I say spirituality

that dwells ...

dwells deep within the very

essence

of each and every being.

But,

alas,

many people do not open their eyes

or heart

to see this truth.

That SPIRITUALITY

creates the power of HAPPINESS

the power of GRACE.

8

A cascading buzz began to rise from the six women, who had sat quietly just minutes before. Then six volcanoes erupted – simultaneously.

Without coordination a floodgate opened and everyone began laughing so hard they practically fell off their chairs. Matie had made her point. She had put a truth out into the light of day.

The oldest of the group, Br'Linda, a traditionally built woman whose brown face was covered in deep wrinkles, spoke up in a full-throated voice, "It's tough to pity them. If we laugh at them for their foolishness they attack us. And even when we laugh with them, we can't be sure that they have the capacity to know the difference."

With these words silence descended as the women continued to nod their understanding of Br'Linda's words. The silence was broken as Dr. Reverend Cooper said while nodding her head in understanding, "That's the way of it, sad, but relevant to talk about."

From Jonelle, the youngest woman attending the group, words came pouring out, "At first I loved my husband. Then I pitied him, like you say Reverend. But then I got angry at him. And then fear came knocking at my door when my late husband, a tall strong man went angry.

"He chose to beat up on me. Beat up on me because I was a woman, because he felt he was allowed to beat up on women. He told me this. I know the world was beating up on him, I don't argue with that, but he came home and took it out on me. Men do this meanness all over the world. They fight, they kill, they howl so loud you'd think they will explode or something.

"And then one day you wind up afraid that they will hurt you so bad that you'll die, broken and bleeding out with no one to aide you.

"Why is it like this?" She pleaded, looking around the room filled with sympathetic faces.

Tonna, a woman who wore no makeup on her face, showed thirty-five years of hard worry and stress as a social worker in the city below. She had seen it all. And some worse.

Instead of looking at Jonelle, Tonna looked towards Nicole, who saw the world through the same lens as herself and said, "It's like this because this is what men are about."

"They tear through the world and leave it in pieces for us to pick up" responded Nicole, the smartly lawyer-dressed woman, who wore her clothes like a military uniform to define her position in the world. This week she sat to the right of Jonelle and across from Tonna.

Diahynne, a good-looking woman in jeans, a T-shirt and boots, sat closet to the Reverend. This was her safe place.

Her hair was braided in perfect rows and framed an oval face with large brown eyes, a long nose and full lips. The combination came alive with vitality when she smiled, which she did a lot.

Diahynne didn't quite always get the fine-print attached to some of the Reverend's words but that didn't dampen down her forging through the intricate, sometimes mind numbing, and yes scary world of critical thinking. It had taken her six months to feel comfortable enough to speak up fearing that the smart lawyer Nicole, would think she was stupid or something.

But once she started talking she found her words were received with kindness and encouragement.

"Some men ain't that bad. I mean they can't all be bad ... not the way ya' all are talkin." Diahynne blurted out.

Jacquelynn sat up straight and pronounced "Hey ladies, my man is a good one. Isn't that right Reverend?"

Matie looked at her best friend and smiled, "Jackie, you're absolutely right, he is one of the good ones, no question about that. And he loves you, no question about that either."

"Well.. OK … maybe there's one good one if you say so," Jonelle said her eyes darting back and forth from the Reverend to Jacquelynn.

"Oh come on Jonelle, there's lots of good ones," Jacquelynn said.

Jonelle and the other women looked at Jacquelynn for a few silent moments, then started to take turns with stories about the men in their lives and the men in the world who either fell into the category of toxic menace or satisfactory.

Br'Linda was the last to make a comment before the discussion ended that evening. She said, "Ya' know, like you were saying, about men doing stuff and women pitying them, and all that … well … I've known some men say they found god or that they go to church regular or that they believe in the good book and stuff like that, but when they at home with the door shut bad things happen.

How do we pity men like this?

"And why do men think if we forgive them it means they have permission to continue being mean and being bullies? I mean … really … forgiveness does not equal permission!"

Into the silence that followed Br'Linda's question, the Reverend stood up, reaching her hands out. Before they grasped each other's hands, to close the circle - ending the discussion – with a prayer of thanks, the Reverend said, "We as women have the right to be angry with male culture. We have the right to be angry with those who abuse us. We have the right, to chuck our abusers out of our lives. We have the right to not allow anyone to abuse us. We have the right to kick-ass."

The woman smiled. Stood. Closed the circle. Ending the meeting with a prayer of thanks.

The world that Tonna , Jonelle and the other women saw and lived in was the arena where the Dr. Reverend Matie Cooper worked. A world pitting spirituality, love, kindness and compassion against reality and religion.

9

Reverend Dr. Cooper had no intention of displacing the "son of god". The man on the cross.

She was a firm devout believer in her faith, in the structure of the bible and in good words and good works. No one doubted that for a second.

When it came to her own ministry (having completed Track I, II and III - and gone through local, regional and state advisory boards - been licensed – and who was then ordained by the Pastor Dobson to preach in the any of the autonomously run Baptist churches) the Reverend Dr. Matie Cooper preached community love and temperance to her flock.

Most of the congregants of the Springrock Baptist Church were happy with temperance, love, hope and charity. Well most of them anyway.

A few wanted the "violent hellfire with brimstone version" of their religion while a few wanted "sinners and winners" sermons.

But everyone had settled for the restrained version upon which the Reverend Dr. Cooper perched her ministry. That is why they called the Reverend Dr. Cooper's preaching – "the kinder version".

Dr. Cooper's "kinder version" was sorely strained at the seams when difficult discussions about race and gender inequality came up.

One of the toughest conversations she had in a group, or privately with a single congregant, was the one about "the talk". From: how do we talk with our young boys - to why the fuck do we need to have the talk in the first place?

Black males are especially vulnerable to the violence from culture, gangs, police, toxic male chauvinism and intentional systemic racism.

Her community understood, as did every black community across the nation, about the "black man driving" syndrome.

And the women understood their men's anger at a world that beats a black man down to the point where their anger, frustration and violence turns on those whom he thinks will take whatever pain he causes them.

Black Women are also vulnerable for the same reasons and from the same sources but they are kept in the shadows. Their lives and aspirations are shoved to a back burner.

Being terrorized, raped, tortured and/or murdered made their life as a black female person so stressful that they die at much higher frequencies, than white women, even from their basic biological capability of bearing children. A very distressing and frightening occurrence that touches the lives of many young women in her congregation.

Patriarchy, hatred, fear, anger and misogyny were mixed up into a toxic deathtrap that was part of Dr. Cooper's life and every one of her female parishioners.

Domestic violence, overwhelmingly male on female, almost to the exclusion of the reverse, is not just a black issue. It's a poverty issue and a cultural issue. And now, today, in her office, were parents who had troubled children, or children who had clueless parents.

10

The Reverend Dr.'s "kinder" approach had especially resonated with Mr. and Mrs. Farley whose daughter, Cayteline, had been dared, at the age of fifteen, into joining a manipulative hate filled gang of her peers. An unfortunately escalating occurance.

According to her parents, Cayteline (a short, somewhat overweight child with a poor self-image and suppressed aptitudes) was saved by the Reverend Dr. Matie Cooper (according to her parents). Now it was their son that they were tearing their hair out over.

"He hates us! Our son hates us!" Mrs. Farley, a tall well-proportioned woman, sighed as tears silently fell down and around her cheeks.

"He doesn't hate us May, he's just … well at least he didn't join a bunch of sick misfits like Cayteline did."

Mrs. Farley turned her head and glared at him.

Matie saw the recriminations coming, so she quickly cut in and said, "The relationship may be strained for the moment but that can change. Just don't close the door. Or at least leave the key where he can find it. One day he'll probably want to walk through it again."

The parents waited. Mrs. Farley holding her fear. Mr. Farley, ram-rod stiff, held his anger and intolerance.

"And … I know someone who might be able to intervene." Matie said, as she smiled and leaned towards the couple in a reassuring manner.

The parents lunged for the lifesaver she had just thrown them.

The Reverend Dr. Matie Cooper, continued to smile consolingly at the distraught parents as they told their story. It was the same comforting look that had helped so many of her congregation deal with the trials and tribulations of parenthood.

Human nature, she would say, "It tends to be hard on everyone … especially the children struggling to grow up."

Drugs, gangs, hopelessness and violence were an ever-increasing presence, from grade school on up, in the lives of not only black children.

The danger had reached into every corner of society, every neighborhood, every town and every city bringing with it death and destruction, pain and sorrow. But, there was never anywhere to hide from racism, bigotry and cultural disadvantages for black folk.

Claire stopped talking.

It's been such a long time, she thought, since Matie's unique way of looking at life crossed her mind. The Reverend Dr. Matie Cooper really was way ahead of the curve. Claire thought.

"DON'T STOP NOW!" Mia implored since I was obviously lost for a moment in a memory clip.

"Ya' know Mia, even though your great aunt Matie had heard all the misery, heartache and pitfalls associated with the "blessing of a child", those are her very own words not mine by the way, she and her husband still planned on having children. She'd been married once, for a short time."

"I knew that. It was sad," Mia whispered.

"Yes it was. During that brief time, she and her husband planned on having a whole bunch of them; like two or three."

"That's not a bunch, that's just normal size!" Mia exclaimed.

"To me that's a bunch! Shhhh! don't interrupt, I'm on a roll here. Anyway, one miscarriage, and, one abysmally incompetent doctor had terminated the possibility of parenthood for your great aunt. And then her husband died.

It was your mom, who has filled that particular void in her life."

"And!" Mia pressed as I took a breath."

"And then, one day, out of the blue, the Reverend Dr. Matie Cooper called your mom for help."

11

"**O**n the day your mom received that distress call from her aunt, all eight of us had been out of high school for six years. Some of us were in business and some of us were still in school, like graduate stuff. Oh! And there were a few babies floating about."

"Like Grace's twins and Whitney's twins! And all four kids are your godchildren too, with the rest of us." Mia almost laughed out loud as she delivered the last bit.

(I have way too many godchildren but at least they're all out of diapers.) I cracked a half smirk with a don't mess with me look and continued, "Back then, it was the hey-day of our trek into young adulthood and we were all making the most of it.

Since Mia had made it known that I was not to go over every single excruciating detail, on Class '94, consisting of stories and vital statistics she has heard a thousand times - I paraphrased.

"Let's see ... Char'Elene had won her Olympic medal, was ratcheting down the competitions while going to medical school. Grace was busy with the greatest little clothing store east of the Mississippi, and Sam was on the Tennis Circuit, or maybe not. Maybe she was doing the store by then. And ..."

"AND!", Mia finished, "Grace had the twins a year after opening the store, while Sam won the money to stock it. Sam had no children then."

"You want me to tell it or not?" I demanded.

"Sorry." Mia said with the proper note of groveling.

"Grace's twins were finally out of diapers by this time. Maybe they were toddlers ... or whatever," I added.

Mia laughed.

"Yes, I have a thing about dirty diapers. And drippy noses. And sticky fingers. And sick kids who you can't do a damn thing for when they are in pain and wallowing in misery. All you can do is stand there like a dummy. That's not for me."

(I don't have an ounce of caregiver in me. Or the need to procreate either. Or the desire to hold my own genetic offspring to my bosom. There's one other like me in Class'94. But we don't talk about her anymore. She's in the wind. That's why we're seven now, and not eight. Ugh.)

"Around this time two of our three-champion cyclist, your mon and Susan, were at college. Your mom was still competing. Scholarship money yada yada yada.

"Actually it was about this time that your mom started wearing her hair cut short like a cap."

"She'll never change that hairstyle." Mia interjected. It's so .... It's so ... ."

"Suitable? Looks great on your mom? And ... she likes it ... you were about to say?" I asked as Mia gave me a get-real look.

"OK get on with it." She said slouching down in my comfortable client chair.

I smiled and continued, "Whitney, the third member of that spectacular bike team, was living in Chicago at this time, with her plumber husband, an amazing child support system, and art gallery representation.

Her set of twins were ... geeze ... I don't know how old they were. All I remember is that both Jeremiah and Eli were also almost out of the diaper stage.

"I don't know if this has any relevance to you, but Whitney lives most of her days in the imaginary world of her art, where she interprets real life into chewable pieces. She is one of the really lucky ones in the world of art, galleries, artists and critics. Not only is she gifted but she has the absolutely necessary litany of support surrounding her. There's a gallery owner, a promoter, a PR/Friday gal combo and a supportive mate and in-laws."

Mia chimed in, "I remember Sam once compared Whitney to a race-car driver coming in for a pit stop. Everyone gathers around Whitney to fix what needs to be fixed, do what has to be done, and then they push her off to keep doing what she does best.

"It's like what all of you have. Each of you support each other. You're always there when you're needed. Well, except for …."

"We don't talk about her!" I snapped.

"O.K. Sensitive subject. So, have you accounted for everyone?"

"Let's see … Whitney had graduated. She had the set of twins. Oh yes, she left the diaper duo with husband and in-laws for a few weeks, because she was in her first group show at some big-time art gallery in New York.

"So … Grace was at the store, Sam on the tennis circuit, Char'Elene stuffing two lifetimes into one, Susan had her degree, your mom headed for her CPA, Whitney was in New York – yes! I said that already" – my answer to the 'are you going senile' look Mia just gave me - and, continuing my thought, I said, "I was doing graduate work and racing. That sounds about right.

"What are you smiling about?" I asked.

"It's just the way you talk about them. You love them all don't you?"

"Of course I do! They're the best." I said indignantly.

"And mom was still racing when the Reverend called, right?"

"Yup. Back then it was Susan who was keeping your mom on the racing circuit winning prize money. Your mom took an extra two years to get all the way to her CPA; school costs money, so she had to keep racing. Susan had stopped racing to be able to finish with her class … but she was still practicing with the team while going on for a law degree. She had to do a loan for that."

"She's a lawyer? I didn't know that."

"She never sat for the bar. If you want to know why you have to go ask her."

"Why are you looking like you want to bite my head off?" Mia whispered.

"SHIT!" I barked.

"What!" Mia demanded looking agitated, maybe worried.

"I need to tell you about Amel'iya, otherwise I can't go on." I'd have to tell her. So ... after an ugly internal battle with the past, I gave in, gave up, threw down my sword and shook my head in disbelief.

(I thought, I really did, that I had Amel'iya safely tucked away in the past - finally. And here she pops right back up. Shit!)

Mia waited with a wary look on her face, not knowing which way I was about to turn.

"O.K. The eighth member of Class'94 is ... was Amel'iya Jackson. Back then the two of us were still going to college and racing together.

"Sprinting for Scholarships we called it.

"Back then none of us would have ever imagined that one day she would betray us.

"Sam says I'm naïve. Maybe she's right. But Amel'iya was one of us. She was brilliant, gorgeous, tall, and played baseball in high school with Grace and me; and we won lots of medals together. Then Amel'iya and I ran for scholarship money in college and graduate school and Grace started her business.

"Amel'iya ... was like .... was like lightening. You'd never know where she'd strike, but when she did it was electrifying."

"Electrifying? The now laughing tweeny said practically chocking on the word.

"You want to really know what to laugh at? Back then, in the time of the dinosaurs, I laughed at the Y2K bug with my sub-set of friends in ether-land. Everyone was crazed about nothing. It was mass hysteria time. But Amel'iya totally ignored it all and continued getting patents and selling stuff I invented."

"I didn't know that!" She was surprised.

"Well now you do." I barked. She pulled her head back into her shell.

"You have no idea how busy we were back then. Getting your life on the road is hard. You'll find that out soon enough."

"It's hard right now." Mia moaned.

"Yeah, but you have a great family behind you." I said rather gently, surprising myself.

"O.K. ... so, what old tunes did you listen to way back then?" Mia prompted trying to keep me on track. Her track.

"Let's see ... there was Whitney Houston, Lee Ann Womack, Limp Bizkit, Bon Jovi, Toni Braxton, Britney Spears, Eminen, U2, Tracy Chapman, Gladys Knight, Madonna and Samantha Munba. They all made the top of the charts.

"And of course, only half the homes in America had internet, and you went to Ask Jeeves for information. There was NO social media as we know it today, No email to your phone, not like we have it today, and movies were rented out of stores. It was the age of the dinosaurs with flying cars and drones way off on the horizon someplace. And you can stop laughing!

"It was school and competition and work around the clock and no one ever slept. Then your mom gets a call one day after one of her competitions. By the way she won that one too," I said to Mia, who had traded in the laughing for a wide beaming smile.

"Well, your mom charged off to her aunt and then the calls for help started to come."

12

"When one of us calls for help we all respond. We've been trained well. And that was due to Elvira Fitzpatrick.

"Ms. Elvira Fitzpatrick, a champion athlete herself, was not only our high school athletic coach but she was our mentor during our four years at Kerry High School.

She was (and in many ways still is) our gossamer winged beatific guardian angel, our own beneficent fairy godmother and the turbine engine behind the powerful sports department of Kerry High School, our alma mater.

During the first week of every freshman class, Elvira Fitzpatrick would cull the freshman class for her potential super stars. She'd been doing this like forever; or maybe like one day less than forever.

"And by some form of magic, only she possessed, she locates the talented kernels, tagged a sport to each of them, and then molded them into remarkable athletes. She is a believer in athletic scholarships and was our primary enabler.

"There is not a one of us, who can say that they would have made it without her. And she is just one of hundreds of thousands of women who came before us paving the road and handing out water bottles to the women heading for the finish line.

"Both sides of the millennium (between the twentieth and twenty first centuries) had amazing women in every field. There were writers, politicians, performers, scientists, lawyers, doctors, entrepreneurs and activists.

"Maya Angelou, Gwen Ifill, Simone de Beauvoir, Angela Davis, Dr Temple Grandin, Dr. Giuliana Tesoro, Alicia Garza, Patrisse Cullors, Opal Tometi, Reena Walker, Bela Abzug and Shirley Chrisholm were but a drop in this golden bucket.

"Class'94, snuggled deep in the mid-west, in a town of black roots, received the filtered effects of these women.

"During our younger years, maybe one or two prominent women registered, with any depth, on our pre-pubescent and hormone drenched brains.

When we started to coalesce as a unit, a group, a talented smart-chick troupe of women in our high school junior and senior years – things started to change.

"For your mom, it had come earlier with your great aunt, the Reverend Dr. Matie Cooper. For the rest of us it was Ms. Elvira Fitzpatrick and Amel'iya who brought feminism and female worth into focus.

"Ms. Elvira Fitzpatrick did it by example.

"Amel'iya did it through the books she read.

Amel'iya always had a book with her when we went to competitions. While I liked Wonder Woman comics, and Grace was into W, Amel'iya went in for non-fiction biographies.

"All of us had gotten into the habit of looking at what she was reading by grabbing the book and looking at the cover (which annoyed her to no end). Eventually she gave up, deciding to just turn the book around to show us what she was reading whenever we passed."

"Who is the smartest of all of you?" Mia was digging

After a bit of thought I said, "Probably Amel'iya. Your mom is math gifted, Susan has the highest IQ, Char'Elene is medical gifted, Sam is what I call a spacial genius, I'm a tech genius, Whitney is most definitely art gifted and Grace has a shrewd head for business but Amel'iya - she just knew everything.

"Sometime in our high school junior year, after we had won an away-game, when Grace, Amel'iya and I were spending the night in an extra bedroom the opposing coach and his family offered for our use, Amel'iya blurted out loud, "A lot of famous black women come from rural. These women went city becoming role-models. Not that they intended to be role models, but that is how it turned out."

"Grace and I just looked at her and then at each other not knowing where this came from or where it was going."

"We're rural," Amel'iya said in response to our looks.

"So?" Grace said, still not understanding what the hell Amel'iya was taking about.

"So!" Amel'iya continued, "Great women gravitate to mega centers of high energy where they have a chance."

"You moving to the big city?" I asked as I dumped my weary body into bed.

"When I finish school. Yes." Amel'iya answered.

"OK... ." Grace who never really understood Amel'iya said, and then added, "just remember to send us a postcard so we know that you're alive."

"I'll come back to see you all. The city is not the outer edge of the galaxy."

"Well, I'm staying in Kerry." Grace stated.

"And I'm going to sleep." I said.

"Why don't you want to stay in Kerry?" Grace asked not understanding why anyone would want to leave their hometown.

"Because real opportunities for black women aren't available in a small town."

"There are opportunities in Kerry, lots of them." Grace insisted.

"For instance?" Amel'iya asked glaring at Grace.

"You could become a teacher or a secretary or maybe even a council member." Grace offered waving her hands around, like what she was saying was so obvious.

At that I peeked out from under the pillow to look at Amel'iya's reaction.

"Say Goodnight Gracie." Was all Amel'iya said as she turned off the light."

"WHAT?" Mia asked. "Why are you staring out into the yard?"

"Amel'iya wasn't just saying goodnight." I sighed.

Mia thought for about three seconds and then threw up her hands. "O.K. what did she mean?"

"Amel'iya was comparing Grace, TO Gracie Allen, a TV actress."

"Sooooo ….?" Mia stretched out the word while rolling her eyes.

"I had to listen to Amel'iya way back in '99, carrying on about the stereotypes on TV, and in the movies, and, how it degrades women. That's when I first heard about Gracie Allen and George Burns."

Mia looked as blank as I did all those years ago when Amel'iya tried to explain the glass ceiling and second-class citizenry.

"Burns and Allen were a popular white couple on TV. Gracie Allen played the part of a woman who appeared as though she was not too smart, while George Burns played the part of the condescending mansplaining guy.

They did a comedy skit ending the program with Gracie saying something that George thought was ridiculous or stupid. He's put it down. Then Gracie would come back with some great punch line, which made the audience laugh, which George had no answer to. She stumped him.

"He just stood there like a dummy while the audience continued to laugh.

"His timing was perfect, he stood still just long enough for the audience to get a good laugh and short enough not to make the joke fall flat. That's when he'd say the one liner the show always ended on, "Say goodnight Gracie' and she would obediently say goodnight to the audience."

"So Amel'iya was telling Grace that she was … what? … naïve? Or ignorant?"

"Yes, Amel'iya was insulting her. And no Grace didn't get it. But then Grace didn't get a lot of stuff Amel'iya talked about. Women's rights, or equality, or opportunities, or autonomy were not on Grace's list then.

13

"But that's about the time it really started for me. That evening, when Amel'iya said she was leaving Kerry and going to the big city. That's when I started looking around my female world for real. Not just listening to Amel'iya carrying on.

'That's when I dug through a used bookstore looking for a copy of Second Sex and couldn't find it, and I had to ask Amel'iya if she had a copy. She gave me one of her withering of-course-I-have-the-book looks, and then let me borrow her copy.

"After reading a few of her other books and listening to some more of her occasional epiphanies I came to a few conclusions: First, no one makes it on their own, never! Especially women. And second, that women enable men in our patriarchal society, men don't enable woman - as a rule.

In fact, I've come around to Margaret Atwood's way of thinking: She said, 'Men are afraid that women will laugh at them. Women are afraid that men will kill them.'

"I conveyed this personal revelation to Amel'iya when we were deep into college shit. It was on the day we looked at the first check that came through on one of my inventions."

"Inventions? Patents?" Would you mind explaining? Mia insisted.

"O.K., I don't know how she did it, but she found out what was needed in the tech world, told me, and when I was able to come up with whatever she told me to invent, she went out and got a patent on it. We share fifty-fifty on the proceeds."

"Wow! And you still get money from stuff you invented?"

"Yes. But that first check was something special. It suggested a way to financial independence for us and that was important.

"I remember telling her that she was now officially - one of my enablers; as I stood there staring in wonder at that beautiful check.

"And then Amel'iya said holding up an imaginary glass. 'We are going to go out and get thoroughly looped and the first drink is to our guardian angel disguised as a mid-western coach. Our very own Ms. Elvira Fitzpatrick.'"

"Then I said holding up my imaginary glass and pretending to clink the two together, 'Amen to that!'"

"And?" Mia asked.

"And that's just what we did.

"I guess you don't do any more collaborations with her?"

"The last piece of tech I worked on for Amel'iya was an Ironkey.

"?" Mia's questioning gaze asked.

"It's a Data Locker. First generation."

"You're really smart you know that?"

I just smiled at the youngling.

She smiled back.

"So, you went out to celebrate." Mia said, waiting for me to continue.

We sure did. And around the fifth or sixth drink I told Amel'iya about the bleacher-bench conversation I had with your mom, about her family and the aunt that she thought was a goddess incarnate.

14

I took a deep breath and plunged back into the past, "It was during our first year at Kerry High when your mom told me something about herself.

"Ms. Elvira Fitzpatrick had us on a very tight exercise and strengthening regime which none of us really hated because we were all into sports, but every once in a while, we cheated a bit; like the day we sat on the bleachers and your mom told me about the day she ran away from home."

"Now we get to the good parts! Right? Mia said impatiently.

I just smiled benevolently. That drove her crazy.

Casey was staring out at the football field but not seeing anything. Something was up.

"During a bad time in my life, when I ran away from home, my aunt came to my rescue. I don't know how I would have made it without her," She said.

I didn't say anything. What do you say to your friend when she tells you she ran away from home? That's serious shit. Even the word run-away frightens me

In the wake of my overwhelming silence Casey continued, "I didn't know much about my mom's family when I was growing up. All I could find out about them was that they were dirt poor, lived in a run-down house on Murray Road; and that they were one of the charity case families in the parish house … not a pretty picture - huh?"

"No. Not very pretty." I whispered.

"Ya' know how I got my name?" Casey said taking a sharp right turn there somewhere.

Cautiously I responded, "No?"

"After I was born one of the nurses asked my mother what she was going to name me, she said, 'Case'.

"The nurse, being a benevolent kind person put a 'y' at the end of my name.

"Case?"

Slowly, Casey said, "For a case of beer."

"NO!"

"She told me she thought she was being asked what she wanted."

"That's ... that's ... I don't know what that is."

"Crap-shit. That's what that is."

"But Casey is a nice name."

"It took one letter to separate me from a case of beer."

I didn't say anything.

This was hard stuff.

"There were seven kids in my mom's family. Five boys and two girls. My mom's the oldest and my aunt Matie's the second youngest." Casey continued.

"Matie got away. She won a full scholarship and left." Casey said proudly, "My mom though was stuck with taking care of her five brothers, a mother who was an alcoholic and a dad who was in jail most of the time.

"My mother and father were salt and pepper. Mom white, dad black. Mixed, some people called it. That was the way people saw them. But they were both black, my mother could pass for white.

"Isn't it funny that no one ever says my mother could pass for black.

"I told this to Ms. Fitzpatrick once, and she told me that in Ireland a couple was called "Mixed" if one was a Protestant and one was a Catholic. And she also said that sometimes people lied about which religion they belonged to in order to avoid the Troubles.

"My uncles couldn't lie though. Couldn't "pass". They were dark like their dad and they had a harder time than my mom did.

"I'm light like my mother while my aunt Matie is mocha, more like her grandfather she told me once."

Casey stopped and looked at me.

What could I say to her? I was just a teenager hearing about the hopeless life of Casey's mom who'd been shackled with the responsibility of her siblings - and parents who were worse than children on top of which they all had to deal with racism and poverty. Maybe not like in the big cities or down deep-south, but black poverty is different than white poverty, anywhere. And it's bad. Plain and simple.

Now, I didn't luck out with my parents either. They didn't know how to do anything else but beat up on me, but Casey's mom was really broken. Like something deep inside of her was drenched in misery and hopelessness."

Tears were rolling down Mia's face.

"Mia ... your grandmother's situation, regardless of color, was not unusual for the eldest daughter; especially of a poor large family. It's the kind of life that decays the spirit and poisons hope.

"And most times the dysfunction keeps degrading people's souls as it's passed down from one generation to the next.

"Your great grandmother passed it down to your grandmother and could have infected your mom if not for Ms. Elvira Fitzpatrick and the Reverend Dr. Matie Cooper.

"The pieces of your mom's story got clearer as we got older. More was added to the story and the picture became even bleaker. Like the fact that the seven kids went to sleep hungry a lot. That they wore Church collected discards and that the tax man kept trying to take the wreck of a house away from the family. But at the last minute the parish priest would hold a fund raiser and the family was given a reprieve.

"At one point the state tried to take the kids and foster them out and put your great grandmother into a state institution; but great grandma took a shotgun to the state worker. He never returned."

"Oh come on Claire, a shotgun?" Mia said wiping the tears away with some tissues I offered.

"Yes a shotgun. That's the way I heard it. And then your mom told me that, 'One by one her aunt and uncles disappeared'.

"Your aunt Matie left on a scholarship to the east coast. Her two brothers ran away from home and wound up in Fresno where they took up long distance hauling. Another brother landed in Texas, but that was the last anyone heard from him. The youngest brother died, something was wrong with his heart and they didn't have the money to fix him.

"Then your great grandma died of cirrhosis of the liver and your great grandpa became a drifter, died or wound up back in jail. No one knows what happened to him. And no one tried to find out.

"Your grandmother stayed on as the house emptied out. And then your grandfather drifted into her life after being released from a Vet hospital. He stuck around long enough for your mom and her three siblings to be born. Once again, the wreck of a house on Murray Road was filled.

"The two boys slept piled one on top of the other in the six by ten-foot room at the back of the house that had originally been a shed. Your mom and her sister slept in a space that had been partitioned off from the main room where they ate, watched TV, did their homework and fought. Your grandparents used the one small bedroom.

"When Casey's dad drifted off into the sunset like her grandfather, she ran away.

"Young girls whose lives have crumbled around them tend not to blame the culprits of their hopeless situation. They tend to either blame themselves or hurt themselves even more than they've been hurt.

"With your mom, it was a loveless home, poverty, hopelessness and heartache that sent her into the dangerous night.

"But, it turned out that your mom was one of the luckiest girls in the world. "

By this time Mia was on the edge of her chair.

"More?" I asked.

"Oh fuck yes!" Mia exclaimed.

I waited with that look I've perfected with my godchildren that read … if you don't watch what you say I'll probably throw you out.

"Oh shit!" she exclaimed to which I burst out laughing to her chagrin. I waited some more.

"Please godmother Stockton will you continue with the story?"

"I don't like the godmother thing any more than the aunt thing." I said with a stern grimace on my face.

With a deep sigh of resignation Mia relented and said as she was counting out on her fingers the number of letters of another word she wasn't supposed to say, "Please Claire, go on with the dash dash dash dash … dash dash dash story. Get back to the bleachers and the run-away part already!"

I smiled, relaxed back into my chair and continued. I get great satisfaction out of winning these tiny little battles with people who take advantage of me. And my godchildren most definitely take advantage of me, as often and as much as they can get away with. Which is a lot!

"Well, your mom was neither lifted off the street, cajoled out of a bus station or molested in an alley. She was one of the lucky run-aways."

"How'd she do it?" Mia was stunned. She had never heard this part. But she most definitely had heard about kids, whether girls or boys, who run away winding up on the streets; and what that meant.

"We were still on the bleachers when your mom told me that her aunt Matie occasionally came to visit her sister, your grandmother. Not often, but enough so that Casey recognized her when she showed up.

"Your mom actually remembers meeting her aunt Matie Cooper when she was three years.

"On one of these visits Matie had come about something important. It must have been important because Casey can remember her mother and her aunt fighting."

"About what?"

"Probably family stuff. But before your great aunt left that time she gave each of the kids a gift."

15

"**W**hat did she give you?" I asked Casey as the afternoon drained away and the sun was starting to set.

"A puzzle book." Casey said with a smile.

"The one you always carry around with you?" I asked.

Casey just smiled at me in silent acknowledgement.

"What's so special about it?" I asked.

"It was the very first present I was ever given. And it had six pages of number puzzles."

"Is that why you're so good at math?"

"Maybe. But I'd like math anyway. It's predictable and logical. Two and two always adds up to four … well maybe not in fractal geometry but even that has a logical progression rationale that you can follow."

"OK … so your aunt gives you a present and then what"

"Then I got the idea about running away. It was after one of her letters came.

Usually my mother goes for the mail, but not that day," Casey said in a voice that told me she didn't want to tell me why she was the one getting the mail, therefore I didn't ask.

"The letter was for my mother, but I tore off the address and hid it," Casey continued, "That's how I found out that my aunt lives in Gening."

"Where's that?" I asked thinking it was just in another part of town.

"Gening, New York."

"New York!" I blurted out.

"Yeah, New York. Upstate New York. North of New York City." Casey answered.

"That's far away," I noted, "isn't it?"

"That's what I thought." Casey said.

"It isn't?" I asked.

"Not after you've been there. Anyway, I decided to run away after my dad walked out and my mom … well my mom started throwing stuff all over the place and yelling at us … and it got worse after that."

"And …"

"And so I took my puzzle book, a bus schedule I got when I went with my brother to the bus station, before he ran away, and then I got a map of New York that I clipped from the gas station out by the highway; and then I stole $182.56 from my mother.

I got on a bus headed east. Two days later I found myself at the bus station at six in the morning in a place called New Paltz."

"Holy shit!" I exclaimed.

"All I thought about was that I was away from Kerry and that my aunt would make everything better."

"Why'd you think that?"

"Because when she gave me the puzzle book, she told me she would always be there for me."

"And you remembered that? You were only three!"

"I remember everything about her." Casey recalled in a far-away voice.

"But you were only three years old Casey!"

"My aunt is magic." Casey insisted.

I just gave her a sideward glance and kept quiet.

"And I saw her a few times after that." Casey confessed.

I gave her a fake punch on her shoulder, enough to push her sideways a little.

She laughed.

"So?" I urged.

"So … when I got to the bus depot in the middle of no place I still had a long way to go. I thought about walking the rest of the way because there were no more buses I could take.

The little map I had, showed mile after mile of highways and bridges between where I was in New Paltz and where my aunt lived in Gening.

You can't walk on highways and I didn't know if the bridges had walkways so I went outside looking for a pay phone and found one. But there was no book to look up my aunt's phone number.

I even walked down the hill from the bus station looking for another pay phone but I couldn't find one, so I went back to the bus station. I took a deep breath, got up my courage and asked the ticket saleslady to help me find a telephone number for my aunt."

"Wow."

"I don't really know how I did it. I was mad and angry and sad all at the same time. And I was sure the lady was going to call the cops on me. But she didn't." Casey said and then stopped.

"Go on! Don't stop there! What happened?" I said a bit too loudly.

"Instead of calling the cops the lady smiled at me and told me, very gently, that she knew my aunt. She said she went to the Reverend Dr. Cooper's Church. To my aunt's Church!"

"WOW, that was lucky! Then what happened?" I demanded.

"Well my aunt came for me of course, and all I remember is that I practically flew into her open arms and started crying."

"Did she send you back?"

"No. I stayed with her for a few years before I came back for high school."

"Why did you come back? Didn't she want you?"

"She wanted me but, there was some legal shit that said she couldn't keep me."

"They made you come back?"

"Yes, but then I met you and I started riding with Susan and Whitney and of course there was Ms. Fitzpatrick looking out for me. And by then I had my aunt's telephone number so I was able to call her whenever I wanted to. So, it wasn't so bad."

"And that's the aunt you go to on holidays?"

"Every holiday." Casey said smiling, "unless she comes here of course."

"You didn't run away." I blurted out as I sometimes do.

"Of course I ran away!" Casey insisted.

"No! you ran forward. You ran towards someone. Run-aways just run. They don't have a destination." I said trying to explain a big concept and get it to escape my teenage brain in some coherent form.

"Maybe that's why my aunt said I came 'with purpose', and that saved me from the evil waiting out there for run-aways, especially fair skinned pretty little black girl. I didn't really know what she meant. Actually, there's a lot of things she says that I don't understand." Casey admitted."

"I think she meant that you put on your - I know where I'm going look – the one that you put on when you're racing. I bet when you have that girl-on-a-mission look no one would dare bother you; well, not unless they were a lunatic or something." I said with a half laugh.

"You got that from Ms. Fitzpatrick didn't you?" Casey said in a good imitation of the stern voice of their coach, 'get to the goal like a girl on a mission'."

"She told you that too?"

"I bet she tells that to all the girls."

"Suppose so. Hey! You're right! I didn't look lost," Casey said in astonishment, "That was up until I got to the bus station. I was really lost then."

"There's always that touch of luck, like Ms. Fitzpatrick tells us. The lady at the depot was your bit of luck." We smiled at each other.

Then I said with what I thought was determination, "I am going to try that when that creep Freddy starts up with me again."

"Yeh, just move like you have a destination, focus and push right through the pack." Casey said looking back at me and we smiled again at each other.

Then I said, "And! I also need to make sure Amel'iya or Sam are with me. Ms. Fitzpatrick calls them Amazons. I bet they could make Freddy wet his pants." We both laughed.

"We sat on the bench doing nothing for a while before Casey got back on her work out bike (her racing bike was kept safe with Ms. Fitzpatrick) and I ran alongside.

"We did that for a while and then she did whirlees and circles around me and we began laughing so hard that she almost fell off the bike. We wound up walking together back to where the road split. One way to where she lived and the other to where I lived.

16

"**A**nd so, your mom hooked up with her aunt, found someone who loved her without reservation. Someone who supported her whole heartedly; becoming her biggest advocate.

"Your mom came back to Kerry, went to high school with all of us - and the rest is history, as the saying goes."

"But that's not all? Right?"

"Right. During college, it was aunt Matie who came to every one of Casey's competition on the east coast; so she could watch Casey and her teammates cross the finish line.

"There was one time though, when Susan, Whitney and your mom were going to be racing in Europe and they were the only black women competing.

"They faced down and dealt with racism here in America, when on the circuit, but didn't know what they would face in Europe. Matie knew this. It didn't matter what else was going on - she was determined to be there to support them.

"Matie wouldn't hear any arguments about it costing way too much. Even then your mom knew what things cost - down to the penny. In fact, after high school, Amel'iya would give her boxes of receipts and our check book and bank statements when tax time came around and ..."

"Aun .... Claire!" Mia yelled tripping over the 'a' word which stopped my reverie.

"Where was I?"

"Europe!" she exclaimed, "Europe!"

"Europe. OK. Your mom, Susan and Whitney were in Europe and Matie crossed the Atlantic for the first time in her life, to cheer them on.

"They got her an official name tag, you know - those things they hang around your neck - so you can stay with the coaches and teams.

"Ya' know, I met your aunt back then. And I remember it because she carried on about food and good nutrition for strong minds and bodies just like Coach Fitzpatrick did. Your great aunt would quote from a Maya Angelou poem. The one about "The Health Food Diner" or Malcolm X's "Culinary Biography – part 1, 2, , 4 & 5".

"With Angelou, it was sprouts versus meat; with Malcolm, it was collard greens, sweet potatoes, fennel, turnip greens, corn meal and no pork.

"It was like getting the nutrition thing from both ends. But they were right. Of course."

"My mom goes at us like that. But not so much my great aunt." Mia said.

"Your great aunt sees what you're all eating when she comes here, and I assume that she thinks it's up to her standards." I offered. Mia just shrugged. They do that a lot, shrug. These tween people.

"Anyway," I resumed, "it was Aunt Matie who came to be with your mom when she gave birth to all you kids. And it's a picture of your mom and dad and the three of you with Matie that sits in a beautiful frame on your mom's desk."

"I love that picture!" Mia crooned as I smiled at her reaction.

"There's a lot of love in that picture."

Mia smiled back at me.

"And now this same aunt, whose your mom's anchor, was calling for help, and your mom headed straight for the airport."

17

"So, how's it going?" I said into the phone before Casey had a chance to say hello.

"Weird. Perplexing. Maybe even a little vicious." Was her response.

"Would you care to be a bit more specific?" I asked and then ... before Casey could answer ... something dangerous happened on my end.

"The phone I was tweaking with a new bit of techgagetry I was testing out, should have made my secured phone practically invisible ... but it pinged.

"Yes, I was alarmed.

"At the moment, the soon-to-be next-generation augmented portable phone I was working on looked like an emaciated octopus with gory parasites clamped onto its brain with an ear piece hanging off one end and a small round disc to catch my words sitting in my palm.

"Amel'iya had wanted one of the secure phones like the alphabet agencies had. And what Amel'iya wanted she usually got.

"She'd gotten a hold of one, somehow - but found it hadn't been good enough for her. When I asked her why a student going for her PhD would want one in the first place, Amel'iya side-stepped the question and told me if I could make one good enough, preferably untraceable, she'd get it patented.

"Amel'iya never answered my question by the way."

"Did you really make an untraceable phone?" Mia said in disbelief.

"No."

"You're lying!"

"No, I'm not!"

"Now I remember! You made something, I know you did, because mom told me that you made a lot of money once by building a super phone."

"A Super Phone?"

"Well that's what she called it. But I bet it was some sort of a spy phone."

"If I tell you I'll have to kill you. And you're too cute to murder."

"AUNT CLAIRE! GET REAL!" the woman-child yelled.

"What did you call me?" I asked in my most menacing voice.

"CLAIRE!" Mia shouted, with exaggerated emphasis, "You invented a super spy phone thing, big deal! So get on with the story, and why did you do it anyway? You were a student."

"For the money of course."

(Before the phone thing, Amel'iya had already procured a patent for one of my inventions setting the stage for our arrangement. Amel'iya looked for holes – NO I don't know how! - in the tech world that needed to be filled, and then I invented something to fill that hole or tweaked something to make it work better.

Amel'iya did the patent work and took care of the business end, which I hated, and we both made money which helped pay for tuition, books, rent, food while augmenting our scholarship and winnings from competition)

"Back to the ping thing?"

"Yeah." Mia said while slouching back into her chair giving me a look I ignored.

"I told your mom, 'Hold on a minute!' Yes I used those exact words. I turned off the ping, checked the readout and said to her, 'Talk to you later.'

"She knew better than to question me when I used that tone, so she hung up and waited.

"Twenty-four hours later your mom received a new seriously expensive enhanced blackberry phone (it was Amel'iya's of course) in the mail with instruction: Only to be used outside of town, out of your car and away from your aunt's place. Call when you can.

The phone wasn't as good as the one I finally enhanced, but it was the best I had on hand at that moment.

18

"**W**hat's going on Claire Elizabeth? This phone looks like some sort of a mutant super techy thing. And EXPENSIVE!" Casey exclaimed, as she parked and locked her aunt's borrowed car. She was going to walk along the path that paralleled the Hudson River, but stopped to look at a tug pulling a barge up the wide water highway.

"Someone tried to use your phone to locate me and I presume listen in on our conversation."

"Listen in on my phone?! Why for heaven's sake? And how can anyone do that?" Casey asked totally bewildered forgetting the tug, the river and that she had started walking again veering off the path and into a tree.

"What's going on with your Aunt? And what was that?"

"I just walked into a tree.

"Don't say a word!"

"A tree? Casey!"

"Forget the tree! My aunt is upset. She thinks unusual things are happening. She can't pin-point anything in particular, but there are rumors and accounts stuff that's not right.

"I came across a few people who told me they don't believe whatever it was that they heard. And when I asked them what they heard they just tell me not to worry about it. But it has to be nasty if they aren't even willing to talk about it. This is just wrong Claire."

"Not nice then?"

"No it's not nice. My aunt is the kindest and most loving person I know. And she is also the nicest woman I know. She doesn't deserve to be maligned by nasty gossip."

"Phony gossip?"

"More than phony ... malicious I think."

"OK, so how can I help?"

After a pause, Casey lowered her voice, "Can you come here?"

After another pause, this time on my end, "Casey!?" I exclaimed, you've got to be kidding.

"Why?"

"You're hours away!"

"It's not that far. It's not like you'd have to cross the High Sierra to get to me." Casey said reassuringly.

"Call me back tonight," was all I said before I hung up on her.

Later that evening Casey called back. (I secured my phone by then. Of course.)

"So?" was Casey's one-word query.

"So, I'm coming."

"Why?"

"Because you asked me?"

"Why?" Casey stubbornly asked again.

"Probably because your aunt thinks weird things are going on. Because she's a realistic pragmatist. And because she's a very put together smart-woman.

"If she thinks there's something going on, then, she's probably right. And I'd come for you which is the same thing as coming for your aunt." After a pause I added way too quickly, "I'm on the next plane out and Susan is coming with me. Amel'iya can't come right away, but if we need her she'll figure something out." I stopped and took in a deep breath.

"SUSAN?! Now really Claire Elizabeth. That's like calling in the big guns to go on a squirrel hunt."

"Casey ... what's in the water out there?" I laughed.

"It's my aunt, she talks in anagrams, symbols, allusions, allegories. It's rubbing off."

"Sounds kind of interesting." I teased.

"Yes, it is, but get back to weird, and how do you know my phone is … what did you call it?" Casey asked.

"Tapped."

"Yes, tapped!" Casey exclaimed.

"Well not exactly your phone. I don't have you wired or anything. But it looks like someone is using your phone to find me. Like they're skipping from you to me, or maybe to anyone you're calling. I just don't know … yet."

"You? What do you have to do with anything going on here? And other people I'm calling?" Casey asked totally befuddled by this time.

"That's exactly what Susan and Amel'iya asked me and I don't have an answer for any of you yet."

"By the way what's Susan doing there?"

"Well, since you went flying off to your aunt, and Susan isn't needed to pace you for your next competition, which is in a month I would like to remind you, she came to check out the legal eagles here at the college. She aced her pre-law remember and is now into torts or something …" I said.

"And she's now wondering if that's going to provide her with a wide enough field to choose from?" Casey prompted.

"Right! We all know that she's decided to marry a judge." I said and sighed.

"I'd bet on it."

"What's so great about judges?" I wondered out loud.

"I haven't the foggiest idea. And Susan won't say. She just wants a judge, so she goes where judges abound. Do judges abound at your university?" Casey asked holding back the laughter.

"There's a lot of law here, but I don't know if they're fledgling judiciaries or judges."

"Judges teach don't they?" Casey asked.

"Everyone teaches. Even plumbers teach."

"She doesn't want a plumber."

"If she did she'd be at a trade school." We both laughed knowing that Susan always said if you want a judge you go to a law school. If you want a doctor you go to pre-med. If you wanted a plumber. Why? she didn't know - except that they make really good money, you'd go to a plumber's trade school."

"See you soon," I said, "and be careful."

19

"That's when it started ?Right?" Mia asked practically jumping out of her chair in anticipation.

"Yes. Before your mom hung up she'd given me a fast rundown on things. Listening to her over the phone, I was certain that something was indeed rotten in Denmark.

"According to the Reverend Dr. Matie Cooper it had all started the day the new Preacher man showed up in town. There was an unease she felt. That's the only way she could explain it."

"Unease?"

"That's what she called it."

"When the man showed up at her church for Sunday services, like the first Sunday after he arrived, and then continued to show up for a whole month of Sundays, your aunt was sure something was wrong.

"Matie told your mom that the new preacher was pleasant to the point of being obsequious and chatted up various individuals once services were ended.

"After that he went around and attended services at all the congregations in the area where black folk worshiped.

When he rented a small storefront for his Mercy Mission Congregation Church your great aunt's hackles rose. Like a warning.

"Your mom told me that it wasn't anything her aunt could put her finger on which infuriated her; making it hard to try and explain why she was so ... ?"I was at a loss for the right word.

Mia offered, "Unnerved?"

"That's it! Unnerved. Like the Reverend had lost her footing.

20

"Casey continued to fill me in on what was going on. She told me that from the outside, the man was about as ordinary as they come. Even if he was dressed like he'd just came off a movie set, He really did look like he was playing the part of a preacher.

"But, Casey said, the only time he wasn't showing off his ordinary good-preacher stuff was when Matie caught him with one of her parishioners, when he thought no one was looking.

"At those rare moments the Reverend Dr. Matie Cooper told Casey that she could see the Preacher's charismatic personality turn sideways, in an ugly leering manner, bordering on passive-aggression.

"What was even more irritating to Matie, was that this preacher man, even though apparently ordinary, acted as though he was entitled. It was the way most men carry themselves according to Matie's keen eye, and at first, nothing really to alarm her; as long as men like him kept their distance.

"Matie knew from way back that young men can purchase authority on credit, for which they are already pre-approved at birth.* Young women, on the other hand, have no such guarantee, no such advantage, no such pre-approval, and, they have a hard time acquiring authority; even when they can best any man.

"*(Nicole Krauss –Do women get to write with authority? NYTimes Sept 24, 2017)

"Matie knew that for a black woman, gaining authority or even enough credit to buy a nice house is doubly hard or not possible at all.

"This dichotomy didn't need a keen eye to notice. It was all pervasive; and it appeared as though the Reverend Dr. Matie Cooper had a lot of first-hand experience with the hypocritical patriarchal system that permeates the world within which all women exist.

"So, the new preacher's attitude of entitlement wasn't all that unusual ... yet it felt wrong to the Reverend.

"Matie told your mom and your mom told us, that the world Matie inhabited, was full of men who don't like women, regardless of what a man might say or how they might act. And these men tend to have an adverse effect on her.

"It was like a bad itch from a raw rash because she'd gotten too near poison ivy.

"But this guy wasn't doing the usual stuff men-who-use-woman do, like belittling, subjugating, abusing, cajoling, pandering, condescending, mansplaining or threatening.

"Outwardly he was the perfect gentleman, so her footing and her judgement was not as firm as she would have liked.

"Especially since the consensus of opinion in town was that for all intents and purposes, he was a cordial helpful and respectful young preacher man who wanted to get to know the lay of the land.

"Her visceral reaction ... which she couldn't explain or quantify ... was that Preacher Charmeur was fishing.

"For what or why she couldn't say. It was just an impression, but one that was keeping her up at night.

21

"After I'd hung up on the call with your mom, I sat there staring at nothing for a long while

"I sat there, swinging back and forth in my chair until I felt someone breathing down my neck.

"I turned around to see Amel'iya standing in the doorway to our cramped quarters."

"What?" I asked rather annoyed.

"So, you're going?" Amel'iya stated as she leaned against the door frame with her arms folded across her chest

"Of course I'm going."

"Without me?" came the snide retort.

"Someone has to hold the fort down here, and anyway you're on a deadline."

"Fuck deadlines. You want me to be here to monitor this monster you're creating?" she pronounced, knowing full well that that was my real ulterior motive. "And … need I remind you … that you are the tech genius and I wouldn't know one end of a circuit from the other."

"Amel'iya! All you have to do is watch for the red light and then call me with whatever the readout says. It's not rocket science. And then I'll tell you what buttons to push"

"But who's going to watch your back?'

"Susan is coming. Remember! Susan who has eyes as sharp as an eagle."

"They're not as good as my eyesight." Amel'iya said stubbornly.

"Well I need those eyes here. And you have work to do. Remember! Your deadline! Now stop complaining and let me show you what you need to do."

Amel'iya went for the last word, as always "If any of you get into trouble, and I mean any of you, you call me. If you don't …."

"Amel'iya stop! We'll call!"

"And you or Susan send me updates every day." She demanded.

"Listen Amel'iya, I don't know if any of my lines to the outside world are safe right now. Someone's got a toe into my phone and right now it looks private."

"Then Casey's aunt is in deeper hog-scat than Casey thinks? And you don't want me there watching your back?"

"OK already! You go tell Susan to stay here and hold down the fort so you can go and watch my back."

"Amel'iya though about this for approximately half a millisecond, looked annoyed and threw up her hands. Going up against Susan, up close and personal, when she has decided to do something, is like going head to head with a tsunami. You just don't win that battle."

"I gave Amel'iya a crash course in how to watch for the red light (which isn't hard) and told her 'keep the place locked up good and tight. In fact I told her to keep the stupid alarm system on – the one she'd been playing around with! "Keep it on all the time! Even when you're in the apartment."

"Yes mom." Amel'iya said plastering her most vindicated smile onto her face.

"Oh shut up!" I swore because she has been on my case about keeping everything locked up, secure and away from prying eyes; or people would steal the stuff I'm working on right out from under my dead or alive fingers tips. Theft was one of the reasons she was big on security. The other reason I'm not so sure about. She didn't talk much about this fetish of hers."

22

After Casey left the house to call Claire Elizabeth, Matie sat in her living room, with a cup of coffee thinking about other bad times in her life.

There are so many dark spots. She thought. I'd been real scared then, just like I am now.

But when you're young there shouldn't be any dark spots. Her anger was rising. Kids should experience nothing but laughter.

Yet, in the real world, she knew all too well, even infants and toddlers grew up with these dark spots; these harbingers of pain, waiting to pull you down sometime in the future.

Feat, terror and all the nightmares that travel with you for a lifetime.

She'd grown up on unkind streets where boys lashed out with the foulest conflagration of dark images they could piece together in short bursts.

A lot of the girls did their fair share of vicious trash talk. It poured out of their anger like red hot daggers on steroids.

When she was young she never understood why they were so spiteful and mean-mouthed. They not only picked on her family but they even tormented her about her name.

Her mother wanted to name her Mathilde you see, because she'd been told that Mathilde was a proper name for a girl; but Matie's mother wasn't sure about the spelling, and she was too afraid to ask anyone. So she named her daughter Matie. Even spelling it wrong, with one t instead of two.

Those folks who knew the family just figured she meant to spell it unusual. The mean kids taunted her about it.

Matie's youth was filled with dark spots.

She'd collected them in a large sturdy box, tying a large red ribbon around the box. She'd put the box on a shelf in her mind store.

As time went on the box became smaller and smaller. Eventually, what was inside didn't wake her up at night in a sweat.

Only in times of great stress did she turn to look at it, as it tumbled off the shelf. Now was one of those times.

She looked down at her hands. They were shaking.

The memories were creeping out of the box.

"Mom, why's John goin' home? Don't he live here no more?" Matie asked her mother.

"Where did you hear such nonsense girl?" Matie's mother scowled to match her harsh words.

Matie told her, "Billy told Mae that John's goin' home."

A sad smile crept across Matie's face as she remembered. I was so young then, barely four years old. I misinterpreted, going down with going home. I didn't know that jail was going down.

Maybe it came from the phrase 'still down' meaning 'down in slavery'. She thought.

She remembered telling Casey about this bad memory, and Casey asking, "What did your mother tell you?"

"She told me, "John is goin' way to jail and won't be home til' yous a big girl. Now, don't ask me no more questions!

And that was that. Of course. She thought. I had no idea what jail was, or how long it would be until I was a big girl.

And, I didn't ask any more questions about John. I didn't have to. I was playing in the yard with Benny the next day and some kid - I had been told to keep away from, stopped at our gate and made fun of John going to jail. Benny yelled back at him but the bully kept on taunting us till mom came out and the bully started to call her bad names. In my four-year-old mind the kid was bad, so jail was bad and so John was bad, and maybe my mom was bad?"

That had been such a long time ago, Matie thought to herself.

And then Matie smiled.

Casey. Casey, the wonderful child, who was growing up into this lovely caring young woman.

She'd made a difference in my life; and in turn, I'd made a difference in her life … just like Father Dobson had in mine.

The Church in all its manifestations was riddled with pedophiles and men suffering from one sort of sexual repression to outright abuse, but Father Dobson was one of those rare, quiet, empathic godly men who truly believed in their calling and who was always there with a helping hand for anyone in need.

He was the one who saw the genius in me. He'd say I was a bundle of pure kinetic energy, a person of moral fortitude, a person whose face and demeanor depicted strength and integrity. He said, I was a born leader.

And it was Father Dobson who made it possible for me to get an education. He convinced his sister and brother-in-law to take me in during my last two years in high school.

I liked his sister, she thought, she made me a nice school uniform. but her husband was a stuffy old curmudgeon. She smiled as she recalled the way he always sat perfectly upright at the dinner table. Eating slow and deliberate.

Of course my teachers began to think I was a bit strange. She laughed to herself. What with all my essays and term papers on theology, philosophy or religious subjects.

The essays and papers were not only unusual for a teenager, but doubly so for a black girl, or any girl for that matter. Especially a girl from middle America Ohio. She remembered.

Nobody paid much attention to me in those days.

A pretty little black girl, wearing hand me downs. She thought as both the sad and the good memories played across her mind. Well no one but the dirty foul-mouthed boys.

She took a sip of her herbal tea, which was just lukewarm by this time, remembering how she had really struggled over the title of one of her essays.

I gave up trying to make something fancy and just wrote 'Why did the boxer dog, next door, kill the young kitten?'

The sight of the little tiger striped kitten being mauled next door to the Dobson's had terrified her at first. Then she was puzzled. There were lots of dogs in the neighborhood. And there were lots of cats. They all seemed to keep from harming the other.

When she'd asked Mr. Dobson, he'd told her that dogs kill cats. But that wasn't right. Mr. Parn, who lived two blocks away, had a dog, who was just as large as the boxer. That dog paid no mind to cats or kittens.

One day she had mustered up enough courage to ask Mr. Parn's why his dog didn't maul cats or kittens.

"Some dogs do and some dogs don't." He told me.

That hadn't been enough of an answer. Five simple words. Some do and some don't. I really puzzled over that one remembering her stubbornness.

"Until I found the word anomaly." She said outload to the vacant room as she leaned back in her chair. What a wonderful word. Anomaly. What a true word. Maybe that's what life's about, a bunch of anomalies.

I still hold with my conclusion, she thought, dogs maul if taught to kill, or are tortured, abused or goaded into anger.

There are also people who kill and then there are those who don't.

Sometimes "nurture turns nature rancid and toxic". Was that what was happening her. Right here in Gening?

Was she dealing with a man who had turned rancid? Spilling toxic bullets her way? Was it the preacher man?

She hadn't told Casey that the first rumor was about her being a lesbian. She'd heard that before. But why the accusations of stealing church funds, or the big fiasco with the bank, or her having an affair down in the city?

If it was this new preacher, why was he troubling the waters in Gening?

In her wiser older years she had come to think that there's always an explanation for everything. You just needed to find it whether you agreed with it or not.

"Need to get some food into me." She said out loud as she got up and headed for the kitchen.

Worry was hammering at the Reverend Dr. Matie Cooper's conscious mind.

What made it worse was that this worry had a ring of steel edged fear forming around it.

23

This wouldn't be the first time Matie found herself in troubled waters.

Just getting an education was a hurdle so high it gave her a nose bleed.

But she got into Princeton with a full scholarship and graduated.

At Princeton, she faced institutional subjugation just for being a woman. On top of that was the race card.

She was the wrong color and the wrong gender; facing personal altercations that threatened her physically. When she decided to go the full course and become a Reverend, only Father Dodson was rooting for her.

Mr. and Mrs. Dobson wanted Matie to become a teacher, like themselves.

She wanted another path.

After her graduation each day got harder and harder to survive. She found herself 'a woman in a man's domain'. Religion. And those hurdles she had to jump were laced with barb-wire.

Matie sat down at the kitchen table with her sandwich and another cup of tea. She took a bite remembering the catastrophe of her first post. I had to resign when I rejected the obnoxious sexual advances from that gross senior Reverend. After that is was like a mine field exploding with male condensation and even female hostility; from one post to the next … until I reached the Springrock Baptist Church.

During those years of practically crawling her way through the minefield that every female reverend faces, she'd become well versed in the signs of aggression and danger.

And once again, aggression and danger were at her front door.

She recognized the signs immediately when some of her parishioners started leaving the Springrock Baptist Church and when others were complaining and even spreading gossip. Or maybe even making it up.

She was under attack.

Whether it was because she was a female in a male's role or someone didn't like her version of Baptist Catholicism, or maybe it was this new preacher man, whatever! It was troubling. So troubling that she was losing sleep and was besieged with headaches.

She had many friends in Gening; many she had known for years, like Jacqueline and her husband who advocated for her to be given the leadership.

But then there was Jackie's father-in-law's hidden hostility towards Matie. He was a thorn in her side.

But as wonderful as Jackie was she was not as expert a confidant as Father Dobson had been. But he had died a long time ago. So, when it came down to who to call, who to trust and who would stand by her no matter what...she called Casey.

24

"It really was a different time back then, wasn't it?" Mia said like she was thinking out loud."

"You bet! In the world outside our front doors, the millennium was about to turn over and "tech driven media" was beginning to exponentially explode.

"Hacking, was becoming a way of life on the internet's information highway, while new and sophisticated programs and software were permanently culling user information.

"In less than six years a presidential candidate would be painting a new canvas on the art of political campaigning.

"The year of the new millennium would be filled with Nintendo 64, Game Boy, Mario 2, Pokémon Stadium, and 117 blood and gore games - like Soldier of Fortune.

"Blackberry had inundated the stores over the past twelve months and X-Men, Dinosaur and Gladiator hit the movie theaters.

"The average monthly rent was $675 and a gallon of gasoline cost $1.26. Vermont passed legislation allowing same sex marriages and Air France Concorde flight 4590 crashed during takeoff from Paris.

"In my world, at that time, I was sure that the world was going to get through the millennium without a massive computer crash or planes falling out of the skies; and, I was sure that I would complete my PhD and win some more races. My plate was full to overflowing.

"And then your mom called me. She had a problem. Well not exactly her problem, it was her aunt's problem. Something bad was happening at the Reverend Dr. Matie Cooper's Church and the Reverend had reached out to your mom for help.

"And then your mom reached out to me. You may ask why'd your mom pick me out of the herd?"

"Because you are her best friend?"

"Nope. She did it because I work in the world of smoke and mirrors, ones and zeroes, mind-bending codes and exponential leaps into the computer tech world.

"Amel'iya severely paraphrased our enterprise for the business cards she had printed for us."

I smiled at the memory

Mia said, "What?"

"Amel'iya said. "If someone didn't know what ETECH meant they weren't worth wasting our time to explain." Amel'iya didn't 'suffer fools'. A phrase she picked up in one of those books she was always reading.

"And that's what your mom needed then. A bit of electronic tech wizardry."

"I like your business cards." Mia said, "It's actually extra-terrestrial like with the ET in the name. And then, it's super-spy cool that you just have your number on the back." Mia almost gaged trying not to laugh.

I looked at her with my sour face and then she did burst out laughing.

(The card did make an impression on those we gave it to, I had to admit; and that's what Amel'iya wanted – promotion she called it. Once you see the card you remember it.)

"Can I get back to the story?" I asked the laughing tweenie.

"You're going to get around to hacking? Aren't you?" Mia goaded.

"You are smart for a pest of a teenager."

Mia just gave me her I-guessed-right smile.

I nodded and continued, "As anyone in the profession or who is not brain dead will tell you - hacking is a very dangerous side effect to the tech age.

"Your mom smelled a rat, a peculiar sort of rat and had decided that she probably would need the skill-set that I had, in order to get her aunt out of the gory maze she was trapped in. And your mom was right."

"So there I was, working away on some problem or other when your mom first called.

Amel'iya was at her desk fighting against a deadline and I was at my clutter-station working – oh yes! I was fluctuating between solving a problem by using hardware or software.

"The first words out of your mom's mouth were, "I'm going to visit my aunt',

"Friendly visit?" I queried Casey a bit hesitantly.

"Nope. She called and asked me to come," Casey said with a far-away whisper in her voice. "She's never done that before."

"Anything specific?"

"She says there's some weird shit going on. Some stuff about cake sales, accounts and dinner dates. Or at least she thinks they're weird. And she wants me to see if the money stuff is fake or real." Casey explained.

After a pause to digest what Casey was saying, I concluded, "Your aunt's fantastic. And possibly the most straight forward person any of us know, well ... except maybe for Elvira. Anyway, whatever's going on I'm sure she's not seeing shadows or making stuff up."

"That's what I'm afraid of." Casey whispered.

"When are you going?"

"I'm off to the airport in ten minutes." Casey said hesitantly.

After a moment to let the 100 mile per hour breeze pass me by I said, "You take care and CALL!" I insisted.

"Yes Mom!" Casey shot back.

I hung up.

Then Amel'iya was about to update Class '94 on Casey but said, "Shit!'

"What."

"Susan got to everyone first."

"And you're surprised? Why?

Amel'iya didn't answer me. She just growled and went back to her brain numbing deadline.

I didn't smile. I was stumped on the tech problem I was tackling and I was starting to see double.

Amel'iya looked over from her desk to mine and recognized the signs. She got up, tapped me on the shoulder and we both headed to our closets to change into our running gear, and off we went for a five miler.

25

"After your mom got that phone call from your great aunt Matie, your mom grabbed her compact traveling bag and headed for the airport.

"Susan only let her go after your mom swore up and down and all around to call and let Susan know what was going on.

"This was not unusual. Susan did stuff like this ... and still does ... which is how the hierarchy of Class'94 was established ... with Susan at its head.

"The decision was set into two stone tablets and brought down from the mountain.

"Susan was officially anointed as our intrepid leader practically from the very beginning. And your mom turned out to be her second in command.

"So, Susan drove your mom to the airport and then continued on to visit Amel'iya and me to scope out the university we were attending for superior judge material."

"Superior judge material?"

"Yes, my little fancy dressed godchild. That's what she told me.

"And like magic, less than twenty-four hours after her aunt Matie called, your mom arrived at Stewart airport in Newburgh, New York.

"Back then, Stewart airport was a puddle-jumper stop for short hops from the major airline hubs and home to the Air Force national guard. Besides the Air Force base in Delaware, Stewart was the secondary drop off point for American soldier's bodies coming home in caskets. It was also where pilots trained to fly C-Class military transports from the C-130 Hercules, C-150 to the C-5M with it wings sagging downward bearing the weight of humongous engines.

"Years later Stewart would turn into an international airport taking the strain off of New York City airports. But, when Casey landed at Stewart all those years ago, she walked down steps that had been pushed up against the side of her small plane. The terminal itself was a small building that shook every time one of the huge grey cargo transports took off or landed.

"Matie was waiting for your mom in the little reception building. When your mom came bounding into the little reception building, it was as if no time at all had passed as they hugged and kissed each other. Their bond was blood and love tight."

"Hey! How do you know that happened?" Mia asked with that doubting squint in her eye.

"Because they always do it that way. We've seen it a dozen times Always the running then the hugging and then the kissing. Oh, and tears. There are usually tears."

"That's sweet." Mia said.

"Yeh, it is." I smiled at her.

26

"**Let's** get us home and you can tell me all about what my girl's been up to these days." Matie said putting her arm around Casey's waist as they proceeded to walk out to the carpark.

After an hour or so of competition stories, Susan and Whitney stories and the pictures Casey had been piling up and had brought for Matie to add to their family album, Matie tried to explain the happenings that told her that she was the target of trouble.

Two nights later, after enjoying another home cooked dinner, Casey told her aunt, "I'm calling Claire Elizabeth."

"But Cas, I really don't know for sure if there's anything going on. It's really nothing more than a guess."

"Aunt Matie, as I once heard in a movie - your guesses are better than most other people's facts."

"Cas, get real! " Matie said with irritation lacing her words.

Casey, smiling at her aunt said in a voice she tried to make sound as serious as she could, "If the man is a liar, a fraud, a fake and a snake oil salesman we need to prove it. Or, if someone is out to ruin you, then we need to identify who that person is and why they're doing this to you."

"But what if he's for real?" Matie asked. "And what other people?"

"Forget the other people for a minute. What's with the hesitation?" Then the penny dropped.

"AUNT MATIE! WHY! Casey accused.

"Why is it that men are usually given the benefit of the doubt while woman are instantly at fault?" Casey asked with as much piss and vinegar as though she were channeling Amel'iya.

"Oh fuckin goat-shit! And here it's me, Matie Cooper, giving this creep an undeserved free get out of jail card when no one gives those free cards out to us women. I should bow my head in shame."

"Fuckin goat-shit?" Casey laughed so hard, not only at the unusual profanity but at the absurd figure of her aunt standing there hanging her head in mock shame that if Matie hadn't reached over to steady her niece Casey might have topple over onto the floor.

Later, as she lay in bed having a hard time falling asleep, Casey wondered, what if it's really a flim-flam? One that isn't all that obvious. (She had just finished her CPA requirements and was about to sit for the certification test, so she was steeped in the two-sets-of-books scenarios. In ways of cheating.)

What if it IS something like a second set of books. He's doing something that looks legit on one end but it's illegal on the other side. The real one hidden away from prying eyes. What if this new preacher IS keeping two sets of books. One for the public and one for himself? Isn't that what con men do? But, why involve my aunt? How would my aunt fit into a scheme? An illegal scheme. It doesn't make sense.

Then there's also the possibility that he's not the source of the rumors and the strange things going on. But then who is? And which hole are THEY hiding in?

Casey kept going back and forth in her mind, is it the preacher or is it something or someone else hidden in the crevices and cracks of this old town?

Her aunt had the feeling that this new preacher man was dangerous. That's a response on a whole different level. Casey thought.

If this preacher man was intentionally cajoling some of her aunt's congregation to desert Springrock what would that matter? That wouldn't be dangerous. People switch Churches and congregations all the time. Even my aunt had to admit that it was not all that unusual for some people to seek out other Pastors or Priests, even other denominations.

But there was more to it than just the loss of congregants. There were the rumors and then there was the incident with the accounts. All told, things were on the verge of becoming vicious. And, it appears to have all started about six months ago, around the time this new preacher man came to town.

And my aunt is really troubled by what's going on.

(Casey had never seen her like this.)

I need help.

This was her last thought as she fell into a troubled sleep.

27

Help was on its way. Meaning Susan and me.

We were on another puddle jumper, on our way to Casey, when Susan became thoughtful, "You and Casey have something in common ya 'know with the Reverend Dr. Matie Cooper."

I waited for the punch line.

"You and Casey and the Reverend Dr. are all kind of self-employed, or going be after you graduate, in a manner of speaking."

I looked puzzled.

"You do tech – and intend to have your own company, Casey does books – and she intends to hang out her own CPA shingle, and the Reverend Dr. Matie Cooper does souls – and she's hired like a sub-contractor (someone who has their own business)."

"You and Casey can lose a client here or there but the difference is that the Reverend can have her contract pulled anytime with the way these Baptist churches are run. Each one is autonomous you know." Susan gave me her-I'm-a-rather-cleaver-git smile.

"Well, NO. I didn't know that little bit of minutia. But, I'm thinking that some of those souls the reverend has sub-contracted to minister to, might be on the wrong side of the 'heaven hell' equation."

"You do have a way with words Claire Elizabeth."

"Hope it's not hell. That would be a bummer." I interjected.

28

While Susan and I took off for the Hudson Valley, Whitney was in New York City at her opening, which turned out to be a huge success. The art world is practically impossible to break into, but Whitney had a sponsor from her racing days; so she was standing on firm ground. (Sometimes fate is funny. Who'd have thought that Whitney's path would have crossed that of an outrageously wealthy art collecting woman whose son was also a racer? As our gossamer winged high school coach would say, "There's always a drop of luck in success.")

Amel'iya was holding down the fort in Boston. She had no nefarious activity to report. Her deadline was almost achieved and the little red light hadn't gone off yet.

Char'Elene was in some operating room doing intern stuff, somewhere, and Grace and Sam were in their store in Kerry, Ohio, (which had been in the black for two years by this time). They were waiting for their updates and if need be they were prepared to lock up the store and head out to New York.

Our plane landed, Casey picked us up and drove us across the river (which I must say I never thought was as big and wide as it actually is) and we were now in Gening; deep in the heart of the Hudson Valley with its gently rolling mountains that had their sharp peaks softened, worn-down and sculpted smooth from eons of howling winds and torrential rain.

It was beautiful country. No doubt about that. The mighty river running through it was a wonder to all who beheld it's enormous width and lush shores.

The river has been the source of food and transportation to the hundreds of thousands of Indian families and tribes that dwelled here for thousands of years long before the Vikings made their long-haul trek over mean waters and wild weather to our shores; and long before the white man came with his diseases and guns.

The mighty Hudson had welcomed or attacked French, Spanish or English ships depending on the politics of the day; consequently being drenched in the blood of the Continental Army and the blood of the indigenous first people.

And then came white man's settlements, industry and commerce; creating fortunes from turning all the natural resources into hard currency.

A hundred years ago boats ran south to New York City on a regular basis from Gening. They were loaded with ceramic mugs, milk jugs, plates and jars all made from the rich clay deposits in the area. On their way back up the river to Albany they'd carry everything from dry goods to imported furniture.

Gening was one of the many towns that dotted the river banks of the Hudson River where everything from hats to harnesses were manufactured.

For people who view the Hudson River for the first time, the sheer size of the river is a jaw dropper as Susan and I found out.

It's a very wide undulating river, that starts in New York City where the salt water of the Atlantic Ocean charges in to meet the fresh water coming down from the mountains up by the Canadian border.

The vista starts with the steep bare cliffs of the Palisades on the Jersey side and then continues on with softly rounded mountain ranges on both sides all the way up to Albany. The river, its views and green sloping ranges has a majestic quality that has inspired painters for hundreds of years.

Casey was used to it.

Susan and I not so much. We just stared wide eyed and open mouthed all the way across the bridge.

29

"From the moment your mom started high school, we all knew that she had an aunt.

"You know of course that Susan was one of your mom's cycling partners (and the most avid collector of information I've ever met). She can pull all the relevant stuff from her sources. Furthermore, Susan can retain all this information without any crib-notes.

"Susan found out that in fact, your mom had a whole slew of relatives. It wasn't a secret. It was just that so many of us had family we didn't want to talk about. Your mom's genetic stock left a lot to be desired … except for her aunt.

"Matie Cooper, was the one constant truest fact in your mom's otherwise tumultuous life. Matie was the one important person who had been there almost from the start.

"But, she lived far away, and like all distant relationships, be them family or friends, they tend to be relegated to the fuzziness of photo albums or a call every few weeks. Life is a busy mess and you need to focus on it, and you need to keep your eyes on what's in front of you. Far distant connections, no matter how close or necessary, tend to take one step behind your shadow.

"These special people hang out on the periphery of one's life until one day they decide to crash the party." I took a breath.

"And that's what happened the day the Reverend Dr. Matie Cooper of Gening New York, called for help? Bad things were happening?" Mia asked.

"Yes."

"That must have been tough on my mom. Getting a call like that." Mia said with a big question mark on her face.

"That's why your mom called us. She was upset and scared.

"This was her aunt, the woman who has rescued her. If anything bad happened to her I don't know what would have happened to your mom … you want to stop for a while?"

After a bit of lip scrunching Mia answered, "No, Let's keep going."

30

The man watched the arrival of the two new women on one of his monitors. Makay'la had heard that two friends of Cooper's niece were coming to town; and she had passed the information on to him probably hoping he's praise her.

He did throw her a backhanded semi-passive aggressive appraisal on her appearance. Delivered with one of his benevolent smiles.

It sounded like a full blown compliment on her ears; even if it really was only a stale crumb. She ate it up like a starving dog.

As the three women went into the house he turned his attention from his screen to one of two listening devices he had planted in the Reverend's house. One in her kitchen and one in her study.

He heard footsteps, luggage being dropped and probably something going on in the kitchen with china and cutlery. But no talking.

And then suddenly he heard, 'Sugar?' it was The Reverend Dr. Cooper's voice.

'Not for me.' one of the woman said, and then silence with more kitchen noises like the cups and saucers were being put on a table or a tray.

'How about we sit in the garden, it's really lovely this time of year.' The Reverend Dr. Cooper said.

The man sat back, thought a moment, and then dismissed the arrival and returned to his primary project.

31

Michelle Goodwell stood at her closed window, in her silent home. Her house, needing a new paint job and a few exterior repairs, stood diagonally across the street from the Reverend's two story hundred year old white-painted clapboard home sporting robin blue shutters, flower boxes hanging from the front windows and a well-attended front yard.

She was watching the new arrivals entering Matie Cooper's house.

Michelle, a woman of average looks, average tastes and average intelligence, with a dark mole at the tip of her left eyebrow, had never been a sweet, kind, loving woman, but neither had she been mean nor hateful.

For most of her formidable years she was possessed with a strong misconception of self-grandeur. But success had never stopped at her door. She'd been an ordinary kindergarten teacher never reaching any high rank in the education hierarchy.

Then her husband died in a tragic crash on the Taconic Parkway during an ice storm.

The Parkway is a treacherous road, built in a bygone age, for vehicles like the model T Fords.

On a particularly stormy night, Mr. Goodwell came speeding around one of the dangerous tight narrow curves the Parkway is known for.

His car skidded and hit one of the stone walls along the narrow curve, spun off, spun around, and came to a stop against the center metal railings.

Why he left the comfort and safety of his car can only be guessed. But out he got, into the freezing downpour.

He was run over. Standing out there on the road. There was no way any of the fast moving on-coming cars could have seen him the cops told Michelle.

Today the Taconic is still too narrow, still with sharp blind curves and is still killing motorists.

Ignoring facts and assurances to the contrary, Ms. Goodwell blamed Matie Cooper for allowing her husband to leave the church that night, after dark and during an ice storm.

She was sure Matie Cooper had sent her husband on some errand that night.

Neither the police, her husband's friends, family or associates were ever able to figure why he was on the parkway. But Michelle knew. She was absolutely sure that Matie Cooper had sent him out there.

(The Reverend and two other people, besides Mr. Goodwell, came checking on the church that terrible night. The Reverend and the two witnesses swore up and down that no one sent Mr. Goodwell on any errand and that none of them knew why he was on the Parkway in a storm with the power of a hurricane.)

Michelle Goodwell kept her ignorance-blinders on. She blamed Matie Cooper for her husband's death, plain and simple, and that was that.

That wasn't all Ms. Goodwell blamed the Reverend Dr. Matie Cooper for. Ms. Goodwell also blamed Matie Cooper for the lust in her husband's eyes when he looked at the woman preaching up at the pulpit.

She would have her revenge. She'd been counting on it for years.

It had already started. Neither the niece nor her friends would be able to stop it.

Michelle Goodwell stood at the window and whispered to herself, "If that Cooper woman hadn't come to Gening, to worm her way to becoming the Reverend at my church, my husband would still be alive

- and doing the accounts at the church; and probably even becoming a Deacon." She was absolutely sure of this.

She went to sleep every night thinking this and waking up every morning convinced of it.

She would now be the one, she - Michelle Goodwell, to not only get rid of Matie Cooper, but to make sure Cooper's reputation was ruined.

Matie Cooper was never going to preach again, anywhere.

Then a cloud of doubt passed over her thoughts.

She brushed it aside and smiled. In case the police paid her too much notice she had a back-up plan. She would point the finger at the preacher.

He hadn't fooled her.

She knew this new preacher wasn't good; but he did know about things and do things that a preacher oughtn't. That was strange; but she could make use of him.

32

What neither Michelle or the preacher man saw or heard was Matie Cooper opening her front door to the new arrivals and Casey pushing her aunt into the hallway while at the same time putting her hand over her startled aunt's mouth.

Susan held up a pad that read – Don't' Talk!

Matie's eyes opened as wide as they could go. But that didn't stop her from gently taking Casey's hand off her mouth, shaking her head in acknowledgement and also raising her eyebrows with a questioning look.

Go to kitchen, the pad read.

Claire Elizabeth and Susan dropped their bags and then they all made their way down the hall to the kitchen where Casey busied herself with the tea kettle while making china noises as Susan wrote – 'ask all of us if we want Sugar'.

And Matie asked the group, "Sugar?"

"No thank you," came the response from Susan and Casey.

As Susan, Casey and Matie enacted the charade, I did a quick run through of the first floor. When I returned we all went out into the backyard.

"What's that?" Matie Cooper asked pointing at a little box I had placed on the small table in front of her. Matie was obviously too overwhelmed to say anything else.

"A sort of disrupter." I offered by way of explanation and quickly added, "so no one can hear us."

"Hear us? Who in heaven's name would be listening? And how?" Matie was totally confused by now.

"Well god could be listening. You're a Reverend Dr. aren't you?" I offered.

The Reverend Dr. Matie Cooper just gave me a look; the kind that Elvira Fitzpatrick our amazing high school coach, whom we all call Ellie now that we're grown up, used to give me.

She's also our guardian angel and used to give me that "look" a lot, especially when I came out with a smart-ass comment.

"Well someone has a camera on your house and there's at least one listening devise inside your home and Casey's phone was hacked." I offered as recompense.

She just stared at me with the cup of tea halfway to her lips. Her eyes were wide open again and going dark. Casey reached over, quickly took the cup, handed it to Susan and grabbed her aunt's arms and said, "It's OK Aunt Matie. Everything's going to be OK.

The Reverend Dr. kept staring at me as though I had two heads or something, and then she blinked.

"I KNEW IT!" She yelled and jumped up, sending Casey falling backwards and landing flat on her rear end.

"It's that slimy Preacher man isn't it? Isn't it!?" She demanded to no one in particular as she started to pace expelling a tirade consisting of an astounding array of malevolent superlatives that were most unbecoming to a Reverend.

I looked at Susan who was about to say something, but shrugged, and then we both looked at Casey who was still on the ground. She just threw up her hands and shook her head.

Matie Cooper had left the room. The Town. The solar system. She was floating out there, somewhere; untethered.

33

I stopped talking.

I got up heading for the kitchen, for a glass of water; with Mia right on my heels.

"And?" She demanded.

I turned around, faced her, raised the glass, drank the water and then said, "Misogyny was one of the trip wires we learned about in high school.

Ms. Fitzpatrick lectured us on this gender trip-wired trap more than once. She'd tell us that women had to work harder, be smarter and have the perseverance to stay on the road - in order to crash through a glass ceiling.

"When each of us hit that ceiling we finally understood exactly what she was talking about. A ceiling that all of us had smashed through by the way, to one degree or another, including your great aunt.

"And there we were in Gening, listening to the Reverend Dr. Matie Cooper speaking about the evils of male entitlement. (Something all men, regardless of race, religion or orientation possess - to some degree.)

"It finally dawned on us, when we were back in high school, during one of our power-runs (that's what Ms. Fitzpatrick called those five milers she'd make all eight of us do on the track) we decided that Ms. Fitzpatrick made the girls work harder because we had to - in order to win.

"Winning would make champions of us, she would say. And champions have an advantage. We didn't really understand this when we were in high school. But, we sure learned it later.

"Either our coach was full of it, or she had a crystal ball because Amel'iya wound up holding the record on bases stolen and I could get to first base faster than anyone else on any of the softball teams we played against.

"The two of us were fast! We worked at it ... we used to joke about winding up 'sprinting for college'. Which in fact we did as you know." I said to a know it all smile on Mia's face as we walked back to our seats.

"Working hard opened the door to our scholarships.

"Looking back, it was our coach who was our first advantage. Scholarships were our second.

"With the additional money from a few patents, our third advantage, we were able to get a better place to live and work; occasionally even able to help Class '94 a little during those years.

"At university I went straight to the top of the heap in computerized technology, programming and design - barreling my way through the male dominated field with tenacity and brains.

"But like all the other female students during those years, I was always passed over for plum projects and the last to receive a stellar grade."

"Was it because you were black?" Mia asked.

"Not only black, but female and smart. Very smart! I think it's a great combination, but it can be as hard as rock in a world bound in slavery to white male domination in half the world, and plain male domination in the rest."

"How did you make it then?" She looked puzzled.

"If not for my support network, I might have taken a different direction. But, I didn't.

"Because, for me, the biggest advantage I had, was the combination of my coach and my seven friends.

"Coach trained me till I bled, made me into a champion and then got me on the road to scholarships. And during the hard times, my friends circled in and out of my life holding me up if I fell down. They were, and still are … the truest sisters any girl could wish for."

Except for Amel'iya. I thought.

Mia waited for me to continue, sensing that I had hit some hurtful thing. I appreciated the effort she made.

"As I said," coming back on line, "Amel'iya and I ran for tuition. For all the other stuff she did the hard work of identifying, patenting and selling my inventions. The patenting was Amel'iya's idea by the way.

"It was one of those patents that put the eye of the big bad Washington agencies in the sky on me.

"That episode soured me to the people who run the government, except for our president, who was the most intelligent put together powerhouse of a woman I have ever met. Well maybe Amel'iya comes close and Susan even closer. But just by a hair."

"The President? Washington?!" Mia exclaimed.

"OH! Didn't mean to mention that. And NO! I'm not going to tell you."

Mia slumped down and gave me one of her nasty looks.

Her sneers don't affect me. I'm impervious.

"O.K. let's talk Self-Employment. Forget the government thing.

"Self-employment came naturally to me, kinda like a no-brainer. Susan took one look at the first check Amel'iya and I got and she gave us some really good lawyer type advice, she told us that since we were now officially self-employed … 'go write your own rules'.

"It was a good thing she told me to do that. (I think Amel'iya knew it already. But I didn't.) You see, you need to know when to call and when to fold. (Yes, that's a song. Amel'iya liked it.)

"The reason I stayed self-employed was not too complicated. It was that many occupations are locked down by men. The field of computer science is one of them.

"I was just not willing to continue spending my life fighting for my job and getting nowhere; on top of which there's the complaints – made by women being harassed in the field – complaints that are swept under the table. It's the bag of shit that comes with "working with men who sabotage and prey on woman."

"Maybe things haven't changed that much?" A thought that bolted out of Mia's subconscious.

"Some ways yes, some ways no. Anita Hill would have made the Supreme Court today. Probably.

"Things are changing. Just not real quick. You and your friends need to keep pushing. Keep working. Keep trying … ."

"And keep voting." Mia added, before I could take that turn in the road. "I know … there's no democracy without us all voting." She recited.g

I smiled.

Mia smiled back at me, but, there was a little cloud behind it. "There's more isn't there?"

"Yes." I answered with a nod, and then continued, "In later years, as I followed my classmates progress, I watched males being basically pre-approved (just like Matie had told us) acting as though it was their birthright, while women were relegated to the outer wings of the theater.

"I kept swimming upstream. Undaunted you might say. We all did.

"I went for my PhD, moved back home, and locked down my town's computer needs. Susan hooked me up with a women's executive organization in New York, through which I was awarded a contract by one of the digital communities in Silicon Valley. And I was off and running.

"And the secret to my success … you might ask … is that I memo everything, record everything and keep a detailed paper trail. This I learned from Grace, and how to actually do it from Char'Elene.

"Male domination (and predators) were also the reason your mom started her own CPA business … which as you know is successful. Her career has taken her out of the wreck of a house where she was born and the hopelessness on Murray Road, where she would have been trapped for life."

"I think things may HAVE changed since you were all in high school." Mia perked up.

"I hope so." I said looking my benevolent best.

"SO?" Mia said hesitantly; her eyebrows climbing up her forehead, making a what's going on face, like she didn't know if I was going to continue.

I looked back at her from my wandering thoughts and continued ... .

34

"**O**.K. where was I?" Wanting to see if Mia was keeping up.

"My great aunt was flat on her rear-end and Susan took over right? She does that a lot doesn't she?" Mia stated with a that's-normal shrug."

I just smiled.

"OK." Susan began … "Reverend Dr. Cooper … please stop pacing, you'll wear out the grass. Come back here and take a seat." Susan commanded as she pointed to the chair Matie had just popped out of. "And Casey, get off your rump. And Claire Elizabeth, you go back in that house with a fine-tooth comb and see what we're up against."

"And you'll find out what the heck's going on here while I'm away?" I asked.

"Of course," Susan said in exasperation

"I disappeared quickly, Casey got off her rump and The Reverend Dr. Cooper looked like a deer paralyzed by oncoming headlights.

"So, Reverend Dr. Cooper, what's going on?" Susan asked in a calm reassuring voice as Casey propelled her aunt back into her chair.

"I don't really know," came the confused answer.

"Well that's not going to help at all." Susan stated.

"Casey. Let's go over what you know." Susan said directly to Casey who was attempting to pour out another cup of tea for her aunt.

Casey then sat back down and began, "A preacher showed up in town. Some parishioners left my aunt's Church and joined this preacher. Some malicious gossip is going around. Some of my aunt's parishioners are pissed off at my aunt about not returning their calls, bake sale funds were missing and then they weren't, and a Church account was closed down at her bank which she didn't authorize. And that's just the tip of the iceberg so to say."

Looking directly at The Reverend Dr. Cooper, Susan said, "Let's start with the gossip; let's start with Nikki Brown, the lady that Casey mentioned to us on the way in from the airport,"

Matie sighed and sat back in her chair, looked around at the two young faces and then began, "Nikki Brown is a very needy woman. She's not very pretty nor is she ugly.

What she is, is smart. But hides it. She's a decent woman who is very malleable. Her likes and dislikes manifest themselves at the polar opposite ends of the spectrum which sometimes makes it difficult to talk to her."

"What does she look like." Susan interrupted and asked in a way that made Casey look skeptical.

"She's just over 5 feet tall. Maybe 5' 1". Has large brown eyes under slim eyebrows. A long nose that flares out at the end, and medium length mousy brown hair that she wears straightened with bangs.

"She gets her hair cut at the beauty shop at the end of Main Street, the one in between the old shoe store that's closed and the hardware store. They can muster a decent haircut, but nothing great.

"I have two parishioners who told me it's affordable." Matie offered in a faraway voice, invoking the qualities of Nikki into some cohesive form for the three women riveting their attention on her.

She continued after a few moments to collect her thoughts, "Nikki's long waisted with short legs and wears sensible shoes and sensible clothes, but they're ugly. Oh! And she walks with a stoop keeping her head down … very rarely looking anyone in the eye."

"She sounds kinda like my mother." Susan digressed for a moment.

"What does she do for a living?" Casey picked up the momentary slack and gave Susan a quick look.

"She works at the small flower shop on Russell Street. They mostly take orders for shipping. You know, those table flower arrangements people send for holidays or birthdays or condolences."

"Has she always worked there?" I asked.

"I don't know. She has a history I've been told, but I've never pursued it."

"Is she still in your congregation?" Susan was back.

"No."

"When did she leave?" Susan asked leaning forward in her chair.

"Matie had to think a moment, "Actually she left about a week after she asked me if I was going to take a leave of absence or go on a sabbatical."

"Those are the rumors about your illness? Right?" Susan asked.

"That's what's troubling. I hadn't heard that rumor until Nikki approached me. And then a week later she up and leaves the congregation."

"So, we have one vulnerable woman who may or may not be the cause of this particular rumor ... or maybe all of them." Susan surmised leaning back into her chair.

"Maybe she just overheard something and misunderstood it?" Matie offered.

"But I presume you asked her who she heard it from?" Susan questioned.

"Of course I did!" Matie answered rather irritated by Susan's implication.

"And?" Susan followed up.

Matie was unsettle, Susan kept her focused, "We were out on the street. It was just by chance that we bumped into each other. After she asked me about the sabbatical, and I told her of course I wasn't taking any time off, I asked her where she heard that. I almost said where did you hear that lie, but I didn't. Then, she quickly said good-bye and kept on walking."

"How about the other people who asked you the same question ?"

Matie didn't respond, so Susan, knowing there were probably others involved picked up the ball and gently lobbed it back over the net, "What did the other people say when you asked them where they heard it from?"

"Come to think of it they each told me the name of one person or another who told them ... and no I did not follow it up. So many people were involved."

"Just one more question," Susan said thoughtfully, "is Nikki the type of person to start a rumor like that?"

"I'd say no, but that was before she left to join the preacher. Now I'm not so sure."

Nikki was in the flower shop putting the finishing touches on a wreath when a smile took hold of her face.

After Sunday services the man had complimented her. He had whispered so quietly that she was sure he had meant no one to overhear.

"You are an especially upright righteous woman Nikki. You are not one of those ugly unholy woman we see so much of these days." the new preacher man whispered as he passed her going from one congregant to the next.

Then her smile vanished, and her eyes became unfocused. Her hands went still as the wreath hung quietly from her callused hands.

She had the means now to get rid of the Reverend Dr. Matie Cooper. And this new preacher man would know how to use what she had in order to get rid of an unholy woman.

35

"But your unease started before the rumors? Didn't it?" Susan asked. "Before that first rumor about your taking a leave of absence?"

It was like a ripple go'in through the congregation. Like an 'unease' you might say."

"And then it was Stellie who first asked you if you were leaving Springrock for good?" Susan continued remembering what Casey had told her.

"Yes … as a matter of fact … it was Stellie who first asked me if I was quitting. And the next thing was really troubling. People were accusing me of not calling them back. Which is just plain wrong."

"Wrong?" Susan prompted.

"Yes. They'd say they called and left a message, but when I actually received the message and called them back it was days later."

"And?" Susan prompted again. Matie was getting lost in her own thoughts.

"And … I called the phone company. Gave them a hard time; but they kept saying there wasn't anything wrong with my phone or my answering machine.

"Late call-backs and a nasty rumor campaign?" Susan said. "This is starting to sound like the beginning of the plague of the seven sins."

"Susan, you have a very vivid imagination young lady. Maybe not plague level, but yes … it was a bit sinful in intent, wasn't it?"

"What next?" Susan asked.

"Then there was the bit about the missing fund-raising money … OH! and a new car," the Reverend said.

Susan looked at Casey who just threw up her hands.

"Car? Susan asked.

"Yes, a car," the Reverend begrudgingly acknowledged. "It was just a silly thing really. Well … that was what I thought at the time. But now that I look back on it, it might have just been another nasty rumor," the Reverend was staring at the blank looks on Casey and Susan's faces.

Mattie gave an exasperated look but continued; getting angrier at all the shit coming down on her doorstep. "As a matter of fact, it was Makay'la who I saw in the market who was the first to congratulate me on my new car. Of course, I assured her that I didn't have a new car. In fact … I don't even have a car! I borrow one on the rare occasions I need to go where the buses don't."

"Why such interest in a new car?" Casey asked her aunt. And wasn't Makay'la one of the women who'd asked if you were going on a sabbatical?

With some hesitation the Reverend said, "Yes as a matter of fact. But this time it seems I was supposed to have bought a new expensive Mercedes SUV."

"Wow!" Susan responded.

"Right." The Reverend said shaking her head in disbelief .

"Anything else?" Susan hesitantly asked.

"There were the questions about new clothes … the dinner down in the city … and a bunch of other petty things. It got to the point that almost every day someone was coming up to me to ask about one false rumor after the other."

"The dinner down in the city?" Susan asked.

"Well there was Stellie and a few others who carried on about a rendezvous in the city and then …," Matie shaking her head in resignation began telling about the episode with Nelson Tenant to the two attentive sets of ears.

"I went down to the city to talk to a journalist … from the NY Times, I might add, who was writing an article about women in the church. He wanted to come up here, but I first wanted to see what he was about. And there was a free lunch at a good restaurant involved, so I went."

"Did he write the article about you?" Susan asked.

"Not about me per se, but I sent him to another woman who is also affiliated with the American Baptist Women In Ministry, and he wrote an OK article; but it wasn't how I would have done it. You gotta be a woman to know. Really know."

"Amen to that." Casey said.

"Susan looked at Casey like she was an alien.

"The reverend just smiled at her niece.

Shaking her head hard to get the 'Amen' out - Susan continued. "That was the only time you went down to the city recently?"

"The only time in the last eight months. Before that it was to attend a meeting of the ABWIM. I was one of the panelists."

To get back on track Susan asked, "O.K., did you do anything to stop this dinner rumor?"

"I gave a sermon on thinking the best of one's neighbors and how false accusations can tear a family apart."

"Did it work?" Casey asked.

"I give good sermons," Matie said which made Casey laugh.

"So, that smear campaign stopped I presume and then what?" Susan asked.

"Interesting that you should call it a smear campaign. Because that is exactly what it was. And no, it didn't stop there. The next bit was serious. For no apparent reason the women who run our cake sale, to raise money for the afterschool program for kids, came storming into my office one afternoon with all their feathers out of whack. They told me that the funds from the cake sale were missing.

"I called up my bookkeeper and asked her to look into the matter, which was the only thing I could do at that moment. I expected her to say she'd get back to me, but she told me right then and there that no money was missing.

"And then she told me that she had also heard the rumor that morning from Jaamika Jones who by the way runs the cake sale. She told me that after Jaamika left her office, my bookkeeper checked our accounts and found everything in order.

I thanked her and then told Jaamika, who was one of the outraged group in my office, that the funds were in the bank and that nothing was missing."

"How did they react?" Susan asked in a manner that made Matie take notice.

"That was the strange part. Jaamika was ruffled that she was wrong. She has a budding case of "pride" that trips her up now and then. The other woman in the little group were looking a bit sheepish."

"So, we have Jaamika Jones, Nikki Brown, Stellie and Makay'la so far." Susan said.

"So far for what?" the Reverend asked.

"Just making a list and checking it twice. Please go on." Susan said encouragingly.

"Plagues, Seven Sins and now a list and checking it twice?" Matie directed this straight at Susan. You're creeping me out."

Susan threw up her hands while making the 'Like what do think is going on here?' eye roll.

"Claire?"

"Yes?"

"Weren't you off someplace doing some reconnaissance or something? Mia asked. "How do you know wh.. OH! You all tell each other everything."

I just smiled.

This time she smiled back.

"Yes, I was busy being a security spy in and around the house. But I came back around the time Susan was collecting the rumors. And of course she filled me in on the other bits later on.

"Class '94 always keeps each other well informed. Don't they?" Mia said with what looked like a genuine smile.

"Yes we do little wedge woman."

"You like my hair and shoes?" Mia perked up with a mile wide smile on her young eager face. She was delighted that I had noticed all the effort she had put into her personal presentation.

"Can't miss it."

"You have that half smiley thing going. Did you just compliment me or make fun of me? I can't tell the difference."

"Most definitely a compliment.

Mia slumped back in her chair.

"What?" I asked not knowing where the mood change came from.

"Matie lived there a long time. In Gening I mean … they must have liked her? Right?"

"That is exactly what we thought."

"But that wasn't the case?"

"Not exactly. She had good friends there, but an invasive species had infected Gening. And it was spewing venom in the worst places."

"Like on people who didn't like my great aunt?"

"A few like that but mostly people who didn't like women being Reverends."

"Plagues, Seven Sins and now a list and checking it twice?" Matie repeated. "Maybe that's about says it all."

"Well … the one about a fancy restaurant in the city and some un-known man was almost hateful. I'd say it was practically laced with sin." Susan offered with a grin. Well a half grin anyway.

"Maybe a little bit of wrath was also being thrown in there some-where?" Susan continued with too much twinkle in her eyes.

"Matie gave Susan a quick eye roll and in a forced even and con-trolled voice she said, "Nikki Brown and Stellie Nelson were the first to lead the charge. First it was the off handed question about my bring ill and then Stellie came storming in here, outraged, early one morning accusing me of …, well is was all lies anyway."

"And the leaving Gening too? Stellie was part of that one. A sabbat-ical if I recall?" Susan checked.

"Yes, that was Stellie too." Matie was somewhere between sad and mad right then but she took a deep breath and continued.

"I sat Stellie down, made some tea, got out a plate of ginger snaps and explain to her that I haven't been to the city for any late-night rendezvous, and that I haven't really had a relationship since getting divorced.

"This was the Stellie whose brother lost the pulpit to you?" Susan asked.

"That's an interesting way of putting it." Matie said. "But yes, her brother wasn't chosen and he left town soon after the board announced my appointment.

"Also, Nikki was to marry Stellie's brother once he was installed. So I'll bet that she was really pissed off too."

"Maybe both Nikki and Stellie think is was your fault somehow?" Susan summed up the situation.

"It was unpleasant. Stellie didn't think a woman should be up at the pulpit. She also believed that her brother was the designated next in line. Maybe he thought so too. And of course Nikki was devastated when he left her here all alone."

"So we have some bad blood here. What happened next?" Susan asked.

"Then there was Chanta." Mattie rolled her eyes.

36

"**Oh** good! You're alone." Was the first thing out of Chanta Blakeman's mouth as she burst into the rectory that afternoon.

Matie, pulled her reading glasses down to the tip of her nose with the middle finger of her left hand, looked up to see the alpha matriarch of the Springrock Baptist Church, elegantly position her posterior exactly in the center of one of the two chairs arranged in front of Matie's desk.

"What's on your mind Chanta?" Matie said opening what she was sure to be a long conversation.

"What's this nonsense that I'm hearing about you're going into the city for dinner and sex … with a stranger?!"

"Not for nothing, but what are you talking about?" Matie responded, not telling Chanta that Stellie had already told her. She removed her glasses which were now tottering at the end of her nose and about to fall off. She placed them dead center on the desk in front of her and then leaned back in her chair.

"I was just told by Alicshia … " seeing no response of recognition on the Reverend's face Chanta said, "Alicshia my housekeeper!" and seeing the Reverend nodding her head in acknowledgement proceeded, "Alicshia told me that one of her friends, who is a parishioner here at Springrock, told her that Jacquelynn Powell's secretary overheard a conversation at the supermarket of all places.

She was told that the people were carrying on about you and some stranger man down in the city. You'd been seen they were saying!

Down in the city! Well I told Alicshia it was utter nonsense and that she was not to spread falsehoods around town."

"And you know it's false … how?" Matie asked with skepticism in her voice.

"For god's sake Reverend, if I can't get you to go out and get interested in my sister's unmarried brother, who is age appropriate, good looking, a successful lawyer, intelligent, charming, a good dresser and well-read then there is no way in heaven or hell that you would pick up a stranger and go galivanting into the city for an illicit rendezvous."

"Chanta, your nephew is an avowed agnostic!"

"Well none of them are perfect Matie! They all come with a flaw or two. I bet it's something to do with their genetic male code." Chanta stated the fact as though it were written across the sky, and as plain as day for everyone to see.

"For goodness sake Chanta, I'm a spiritual person."

"Of course you are."

Your nephew's a heathen."

"So?"

"A non-believing radical-agnostic?"

Chanta just looked at Matie as though this was all irrelevant.

"And, by the way, he's also a cynical anti-spiritualist. He's the poster boy for 'There's No God In Heaven Club'."

"Matie! Chanta repeated exasperated, "None of them are perfect! They're men!"

Instead of getting stuck in this loop about male imperfection, the Reverend Dr. Cooper changed the course of the conversation and said, "What's interesting is that you believe the gossip is false because you can't set me up? And god knows you've tried long and hard … that is interesting reasoning."

"Well it's true! And if you're saying it's not true then god didn't make little green apples."

"You're quoting Robert Russell today?"

"It was a great song." Chanta's bruised ego pouted.

'Yes, Chanta it was a great song and yes you are right. I didn't go galivanting off to the city for an outrageous dinner and wild sex."

"There are times I wish that you did. A life of celibacy is just plain wicked." She slumped slightly giving way to resignation, but then quickly straightened herself back up into her normal balance.

With that Matie Copper burst out laughing and so did the very fix-it-all outspoken matriarch of the Springrock Baptist Church.

37

Matie looked at both Casey and Susan after telling them this last bit and said, "When I came home that evening I realized that I wasn't just being harassed with innuendoes. My good name had become center mass on a big target board.

"The target insinuated that I was not fit for my job.

"My reputation was being ripped to shreds."

After a moment of silence, the Reverend said lowering her voice, "It was all lies, the lot of it."

"A heathen non-believing radical- agnostic … cynical anti-spiritual-ist?" Susan asked with mischief in her voice.

"She has a super-charged memory," Casey explained to her aunt who was amazed at Susan's exact recall.

"Don't forget the poster boy for 'There's No God In Heaven Club'." Susan said, and then added, "OK Ladies! What we have here is plain and simple character assassination. Almost biblical in proportions... ya' know, like wrath, envy, some pride and hubris thrown into the cal-dron." Susan was attempting to pull all the threads together, "and then there is the account thing that Casey told us about.

"But WHY? It just doesn't make any sense."

Susan didn't answer. A cold wind blew in from where nasty cold winds blow in from and the mood in the room changed.

The Reverend Dr. Cooper's mood changed precipitously. Like it dropped fifty degrees instantaneously.

"What if this unknown person, if there is such a person, digs into my family history? I have people in my family who've gone to jail or skipped the going to jail part and took off. Relatives who basically were criminals or … ." Matie stopped mid-sentence.

"If all this is being directed at me, to hurt me, or cause me to lose my position here, then a few bits of red meat thrown around … like - maybe one day I'll run away with all the Church funds - could be toxic. Maybe that was what the lavish dinner was all about. Maybe the car, the expensive clothes and jewelry are hints of ill-gotten gains?"

"Stop that Aunt Matie," Casey snapped. "Stop that right now!"

Everyone became silent.

The silence disturbed Reverend Cooper's tabby cat. She stretched out on the fence rim, looked over at the group of women waiting for life to continue in it's normal chaotic tempo.

A slight afternoon breeze brought with it the scent of cooking from somewhere in the neighborhood.

Breaking the silence Susan asked, "Are Stellie, Jaamika, Makay'la and Nikki still in your congregation?"

"As a matter of fact they all left, and another six parishioners, some women some men, have gone over to the preacher man too. I don't know yet how many others from the full congregation, the ones I don't see very often, who might have also gone over to the preacher."

"So that's a yes? Stellie, Jaamika and Nikki are part of the ten little Indians?" Susan asked to make sure her list was accurate.

"Are you going Agatha Christie on us?" Casey asked.

"Well this is sort of a mystery." Susan said in her defense.

"One of my congregants also likes to talk in quotes from her favorite books. And no, before you ask, she is still at Springrock and she's also thoroughly pissed off at the secret rendezvous gossip, just like Chanta Blakeman."

Susan continued, "Why do you say gone-over to the preacher?"

"It's just an expression from our past. It's a cryptic way of saying traitor or turncoat." We all nodded our heads.

Occasionally I have a congregant switch to one of the other houses of worship in the area, but all the congregants, who recently left Springrock, joined the preacher's congregation."

38

"That's why my aunt called me." Casey broke in, "All this strange stuff happening; like one thing after the other. That's why I came out here to see if I could help her out. Especially about the bank."

"I know you've probably gone over it a dozen times, but if you can just do it one more time." Susan looked at the reverend.

"The bank said I'd transferred an enormous amount from the church funds into my personal bank account.

"Before you ask - Yes, I protested.

"Yes, the bank checked.

"There was nothing wrong with the transaction, other than I didn't do it." The Reverend stated.

"Who checked it out for you? I mean this is serious!" Susan demanded.

"The bank manager herself. They don't have a bank president anymore." Matie sighed.

"So, she didn't have an expert check it out? Like a forensic accountant," Susan asked the Reverend and then snapped her head to the left as Casey said, "No!"

"And you went … with your aunt … to the bank to try and check this out?" She asked Casey.

"Yes of course I did! I told you that. And they wouldn't give me access. The manager just threw some gobbledy gook at me about lawyers and the privacy of all their clients stuff. And I threw around some credential stuff but that didn't make any difference. The best that

I could do was to fill out all the papers requesting a deep search on the account."

"So, no forensic accountant." Susan stated the obvious looking at Casey.

The Reverend disbelieving the avenue this conversation was taking said, "I don't even think they have one. At least the bank manager never said anything about one."

"So, no one went digging into the issue?" Susan asked.

"We haven't heard back, and, as far as I know they're not going to do any digging as you say," the reverend said through tight lips.

We waited.

"I was given a printout of the transaction. It even looks legitimate to me. But I didn't make it!" Matie repeated, "Oh! And the bank manager, who I personally am acquainted with, acted as though it was my fault. Like I was half-way to an old age home or something. I can tell you that it was strange being treated like a non-sensible woman by another woman.

"It's one thing when I get this condensation from a man, but I never can get used to it coming from a woman.

The next day when I called the main office to talk to a supervisor he had the nerve to say, 'Reverend Cooper, high finance can be a bit tricky for women, especially with computers these days'. And before he could insult me any more I made it very plain to him that I was more than capable of dealing with large funds, complicated finances, grants and projects; more so than he was, and then I hung up on him."

"What happened to the account?" Susan asked raising her eyebrows at the retort.

"The next day the manager called and apologized and said everything had been corrected and if I had any further problems to call her. It was the usual bullshit."

"Ouch," Susan said.

"And no explanation." Casey added.

"And now you tell me someone might be spying on me or stalking me or both?" Reverend Dr. Cooper asked. There was a tremble in her voice.

"Aunt Matie?" Casey said breaking into the conversation, determined to turn her aunt's attention to something concrete.

Matie turned her focus onto her niece.

"I'd say this all adds up to weird. Too weird," Casey offered.

Before Matie could answer I returned. All eyes fell on me.

39

"Reverend Dr. Cooper, here's what we're going to do", I said as I walked over to the Reverend. "and you need to follow my instructions to the letter. Also, you are not to tell anyone, absolutely no one what you are doing. And I mean no one." I added for emphasis in a clipped no nonsense voice. (The day had gotten longer and we really needed to get over to Matie's office)

"Am I in trouble?" the Reverend asked in a shaky voice, "you're scaring me."

"I'm sorry. I don't know, exactly, yet, if you're in trouble and I don't mean to scare you. But, before you pelt me with question, someone has you targeted, for some reason that I don't know yet."

I turned my attention towards Susan and asked, "Any thoughts?"

"I'd say someone has it in for our dear Reverend Dr. Cooper." Susan offered. "This includes: four women we know about and a few men, to be looked at later who have gone over into the enemy's camp. Reason unknown. Oh! And maybe this new so called preacher man. Why he'd be after the Reverend? Unknow. Maybe it's all him, maybe not."

So, we got to work.

First, we scripted a dialogue that we'd use when we returned to the house.

Whenever we wanted to have a real conversation – the disruptor – my name for my little black box, would be activated. No ands ifs or buts I told Matie.

Susan and Casey were going to make a stop at one of the new preacher's sermons, with the excuse that Casey found the current Mercy Mission project something she'd like to bring back to her Church in Boston (no she didn't have a church in Boston). And I went with Matie to her Church office and went through the rectory with a fine-tooth comb, bringing my bag of assorted equipment, including instruments to check for bugs of all kinds.

Nothing showed up.

"If your house is bugged then this place also has to be bugged. It may not actually be activated at the moment." I said more to myself than to anyone else in the room.

While I was checking out the office, Susan and Casey came back and Susan and Matie walked through the Church, Matie being the guide.

While the rest of us were occupied, Casey looked at the books lining a whole wall of the room.

OK," I said to myself, "time to dismantle."

And with that my tools appeared, and I dove into the Church's computer. It was one of the first commercialized ones. Almost like a fancy word processor. But it had a connection to the fledgling internet. And it was sophisticated enough for hackers and unregulated enough so they were practically invisible.

Just as Matie and Susan finished their little tour, I said," You're just in time."

Matie and Susan followed my finger pointing at something in the guts of the opened computer.

"What's that?" Matie asked.

"A relay." I answered.

Matie just looked blank and shook her head.

"Basically, it allows an outsider to watch everything you do on your computer. Now all we need to do is find the transmitter."

Matie almost collapsed.

If Susan hadn't directed her sagging body into the nearest chair the Reverend would have landed in a heap at their feet.

"Someone bugged my computer?" Matie asked incredulously with her head hanging down in her hands.

From across the room Casey said, "Well well, lookey here."

"What now?" Asked a frazzled Reverend lifting her head.

"I found a bible.'"

"Cas, that might not be considered unusual in a Church," Susan said sarcastically.

Matie jumped up and came over to Casey, who had the back cover opened. Matie flipped the cover closed over Casey's finger and turned the book to look at the front cover.

"It's a bible all right. So?" Matie asked deflated.

"Is it yours?" Casey asked in a way that told Matie she had missed something important.

Matie took another once over - even though Casey was still holding the book, and still had her finger inserted under the back cover.

"Actually, it's a common enough bible, I have a few exactly like this one here on the shelves, but it shouldn't be on this shelf." Matie said giving Casey a questioning look.

By this time both Susan and I had joined, as the audience.

"OK smarty, what'ya got?" Susan asked.

Slowly Casey opened the back cover again and held the book up length wise so we could all see the thick back cover.

I reached out and ran my fingers over both sides.

"How in heavens name did you pick this one out of the hundreds here?"

Not getting an answer, Susan insisted, "Will someone tell me what's going on with this bible?"

"I think our super sleuth Casey here has found our transmitter. And, she is going to tell us how she spotted it."

"Oh my goodness!" exclaimed Casey's aunt, "It's not in order."

"You alphabetize your books?" Both Susan and I exclaimed in unison.

"Not the alphabet. Don't be silly. It's by dates! Which is the way my aunt prefers to keep her large collection of Bibles. And I've helped my aunt redo these shelves more times than I can remember during the time I was here as a little girl." Casey said smiling at her aunt.

"And if this one were one of mine, it would be on a different shelf." Matie said giving her niece a sideward hug, "And you remembered."

Susan and I looked at each other and smiled. We were all smiling. That's good. Especially when things are really weird ... like probably dangerous weird.

"OK." I said interrupting the family moment, "before we go any further, I'm going to put the computer back as I found it, and Reverend, you are not to use it unless I say you can, and I'm going to the bank. So, let's sit you down at your desk and write me out a permission slip to go barging into your accounts at the bank."

"But I've already done that," Matie said.

"I'm talking deep forensic back door stuff. Hidden things that don't show up unless you know how to look for it."

"You can do THAT! And.. are they just going to let you just go into all the secure and private stuff? WHO are you?"

"I'm the person who's going to get Casey what she needs to figure out what's going on." I said to Matie's unbelieving face.

"O.K.," I said trying to calm Matie down, "I have this friend who is going to help me with getting the creds I'll need."

"Matie looked at me with that OK you told the truth this time look, and Casey asked, "Who!"

40

"**A** few years back, somewhere between my masters and my soon to be PhD, I met David Hathaway. (I was rudely recruited (kidnapped is more like it) and dumped into the Washington alphabet menagerie for a one-time job.)

"One of the conditions I insisted on (before accepting the job, and before I was deposited somewhere secret) was that my identity and involvement would be wiped off their conscious mind.

"When I was finished no one was ever to know I was there; that was my plan. (Why? You might ask. Well it's not healthy getting too close with what goes on behind closed doors in the WDC world.)

"Other than the President, who gave me a really cool get out of jail card, if I ever needed it, there was David Hathaway on the other end of the super spy sat phone I was given.

(I used the phone only once. It was an emergency! O.K.! There were bad guys all around and we needed to protect all my godchildren. Of which I have way too many. Anyway, David insisted that I maintain some link, just in case. So I still have the phone.)

"Why the phone," I had asked David the day he handed it to me.
"Just in case."

"Just in case of what?" I asked … knowing that I probably was not going to like the answer I most certainly was going to be given.

"In case we haven't deep sixed your cover sufficiently. In case you are approached by foreign nationals for nefarious purposes. In case you decide to come back and work for us."

"I don't like any of those reasons!" The first and the second scared the shit out of me; and the third one made me nauseous.

"Well you are in the best and brightest category. We can't hide that completely." David said.

(I had nothing to come back with to that. And now, here I was calling him for forensic creds to go into bank records without any real evidence that a crime was or is being committed.)

"Hi there Ms. Stockton." David said. (like it hadn't been years since we spoke to each other) "What brings you to my doorstep. Metaphorically speaking that is," came the friendly voice of David Hathaway over the sat phone.

"I could use a little bit of help breaking into bank records- in order to see if my friend's aunt's identity has been stolen or whether or not it's being used to ruin her." I blurted out before I changed my mind. "And ... I need some super over the top creds that will allow me to look into the eye of the big bad bank monsters without setting off outrage and chest thumping."

"And I'm to help you? Why?" David asked.

"Because stuff like this may be happening all over the place. And because, if my suspicions are right, it means we have a talented criminal hacker here whose up to no good. And don't forget the millennium bug that might be out there. This may be connected."

"There is no bug out anywhere, but I'm always interested in the various incarnations in the criminal world, especially the tech world. So, tell me what's going on."

"Of course there's a bug. There are millions of them, even I ..."

"And you called me to start an argument about bugs? Or to tell me you have created one?"

I clamed up with that and went directly to my story.

Afterwards, David asked, "You say your Reverend has identified at least ten people who've deserted her church, so far, plus the new preacher of course; do you have a list?"

"Susan does. I'll get it from her and send it to you. And ... if you see anything unusual while we're in, you will let me know? Right! I'm assuming here that you'll be looking over my shoulder?"

"Yes I will be looking over your shoulder. No, I will not tell you if one of them is in the WPP or undercover." David answered in his most serious tone.

"David! Why would the Fibs put anyone into the witness protection program here in a little town in New York? And undercover cops? What've you been smoking lately?"

"Hey! Stranger things have happened."

"David!"

"Yes?"

"You can be a jerk sometimes you know."

"And you want my help?"

"Of course!" Was the only answer he was getting.

I could see him smiling, but I wasn't going to tell him that.

"I'm sending the creds up by special messenger, should be there tomorrow morning. And when you get in, tie me in, invisibility pre-ferred, so we can both snoop."

"Are you allowed to do that in a private account without a warrant?"

"You have the account holder's permission I presume?"

"Yes."

"And I have cause to think we have criminal activity going on...so."

"So, we're covered," I said smiling.

"You're smiling." David said.

"I'm hanging up." Which is exactly what I did.

"You know I'm still here? Right?" Mia asked.

"Was I wondering off?"

"Spy stuff, satellite phones and the president of the United States! Yeah! You were wondering off. Like totally off the tracks."

"What?" I asked the quizzical look on Mia's face. She was high end skeptical at this point.

"It's all true?" I insisted.

"All I can say is that's how I got the creds that I needed when I showed up at Matie's bank the minute it opened the next day.

"Much to the strong disapproval of the manager and the many road-blocks the bank's corporate legal suits put up that morning. But, by noontime I was in. And now I was miles deep in data minutiae.

"What I was looking for though was the trick door, the splice, the incursion, the hack. What Casey would be looking for was the 'Who' and 'Why'."

41

Casey and Susan went scavenging.

"Are you the Reverend Cooper's niece?" came a breathless woman's voice behind them.

"Yes I am," Casey said.

"I thought so. I saw you at the grocery store with Reverend Cooper last week when you were introduced to the store owner."

So, she didn't have to ask? She knows who we are. Casey's eyes said to Susan who nodded.

"I'm so glad you came today. Are you interested in our Mercy Missions?" Jaamika Jones asked.

"Actually I am," Casey said,

"Oh, that is wonderful. Preacher Charmeur will be so pleased. Let me introduce you."

"She's been sent to deliver us," Susan whispered into Casey's ear as they followed the woman back up the center aisle.

Well?" how did it go?" Matie asked as soon as she came home from her Sunday service and bible study at Springrock.

"The man is good," Susan said having made sure that the contraption Claire Elizabeth had brought to scramble all sounds in the house was glowing green.

"Apparently, he only collects small amounts for the Church, the seeds, the books, the pencils, the wells and doesn't appear to be fleecing anyone." Susan sighed.

"He's not an NGO, a registered charity or a philanthropy." Casey added.

"He's just a regular guy doing good works for god and the human race." Susan added, putting out the plates for lunch.

"He looks legit but I can't be sure until I get a look at his books and that's not likely to happen. And anyway, he doesn't have to account for the money that is donated to his Mercy Projects, which by the way Jaamika Jones calls their Mercy Missions." Casey said waving her aunt over to the table.

"How can that be? My bookkeeper has to account for every penny that comes into the Church!" Matie asked sitting down at the round oak table.

"In a nutshell, the money is considered gifts to him personally. He can do as he pleases. And he does have this very impressively leather-bound book, with a gold cross on the black cover …" Casey said as her aunt interrupted.

"But …" Matie started to say.

"Gifts are gifts aunt Matie, and he's up front with his congregation." Casey said.

"They all seem to think his method of collecting money is some way to beat taxes and use every penny for their Mercy Mission projects, or the rent and lights; oh, and to put a few dollars into the Preachers pocket 'but the man has to eat' I was told." Susan said.

"Where did you hear this, that's outrageous. We're all tax exemp … Oh!" Matie said deflating.

"That's right aunt Matie, you're legit, he's just your average …. " Casey started to say but caught herself before some really foul language escaped into the room.

"Oh, and the best part! The Preacher tells us that he only collects what people can afford for the Mercy projects." Susan offered.

With a straight face, he told us that fifty cents is just as powerful as a dollar in god's eyes." Casey said.

"So, if he's not actually fleecing all the people who've joined his so-called congregation, then maybe he isn't the person targeting me.

Maybe we're looking in the wrong direction?" Matie said a little hesitantly.

"Is there something else?" Casey asked her aunt.

"Some mumblings from my staunchest supporters about discord."

"Today?"

"Yes, after services. It's nothing anyone can point a finger to, just that they like their Reverends to not make waves."

"But you push the envelope every time you have one of your discussion groups and sometimes even with your sermons."

"That's expected. Controversy over funds that are missing one minute and not the next is another matter altogether. And then there's that car and all the other stuff." She moaned.

"So, we need to get to the bottom of this - fast." Susan said looking straight at Casey and me.

The Preacher had just finished a very satisfying meal at one of his parishioner's homes and was saying his good-byes when Jessea Baret, another convert from Springrock, said, "That sweet little relative of Reverend Cooper gave us a five-dollar donation for our education project."

The Preacher, put his hand gently on Jessea's shoulder and with a calm beatific smile on his face said, "That was very generous of her. Very generous indeed. Her sins, or the sins of her aunt must be mighty big to warrant a five dollar bill."

When he looked straight into her eyes, as though no one else in the world existed, Jessea Baret would have said anything, done anything for the man.

Jessea Baret was nodding her head in agreement at his words. "There's sins aplenty there."

"As you say sister Jessea, 'sins aplenty there."

Jessea Baret was cut from the same cloth as his other recruits.

He was a Preacher to them. With bonafides and ordained (a lie, that they believed). They also believed with their whole being that a Preacher (or even the white pope) belonged to god, so, a Preacher knows what's right and what's wrong, therefore, they follow and do his bidding blindly … with verve.

The simplicity of unadulterated ignorance and how to use it for a hornswoggle flim-flam by a smart con-man was the cesspool the preacher swam in.

And smart he was.

This HE truly believed.

That afternoon Charmeur checked his books. In the six months he'd been here he'd pulled in ten thousand, six hundred and eighty-two dollars. The seeds cost four hundred dollars, and the first surface well had been completed for twelve hundred dollars.

Then there was rent for the storefront on main street, that held his fifty soft souls, that was four hundred and fifty dollars a month. In all appearances, he seemed to be an honest, frugal, above-board man. A man of good intentions doing god's good works.

Then he opened his computer to his other world.

He turned on the relay giving him access to Matie Cooper's office.

Her computer was off.

He then went to his audio devises. There was some sort of static interference. He frowned. He checked his end, but it was something else. He sat there listening to the soft confusion of sound and wondered what the problem could be.

Just then the sound of woman's voices came over his speaker. All gibberish he concluded.

He smiled to himself. His spying could continue. He was good. So now to hook the big fish.

42

"Your mom was back plowing through the piles of info I'd given her looking for a thread to pull.

Then she found it and started to pull.

Now she was giving me instructions that were focused and specific.

"By the way your mom is the "Number one Hound dog of numbers". She gets the scent, puts nose to ground, and follows the trail relentlessly."

Mia smiled knowing what I was talking about.

"So there I was, busy gathering and hunting. And Susan, who'd been out and about in Gening, came storming back into Matie's house to deliver an astonishing bit of news.

Another rumor. But this one could cost the Reverend Dr. Cooper her ministry license."

(What I didn't know at that precise moment, but of course was to learn before Susan was done was - in the worldwide organization of Baptist Churches, each Baptist Church/congregation is an autonomous entity, responsible for governing itself. Any individual Baptist Church, like Matie's Church, can revoke the license of a Reverend/Pastor.

The sort of ignorant gossip, driven by fear, hatred or even jealousy, or a scheming con-man could put the Reverend Dr. Matie Cooper's life's work on shaky ground.)

"Susan had heard this latest rumor while engaged in what Casey teased her as reconnoitering but what I call spying. She ignored both jabs expertly bringing back bits and pieces of the puzzle each day.

She'd ask a casual question in one place and make a remark in another, both of which started a conversation that ultimately wound up with town gossip. Susan had the uncanny ability of being able to squeeze information out of a dried-up turnip green.

When the word coven hit Susan's ears it was like being hit over the head with a sledge hammer.

She'd been walking the aisles of the town's one and only super-market, hunting for the right person to start up a conversation with - when she overheard two woman talking.

"Coven?!" Casey immediately questioned, not sure that her ears were working.

"Yes. Coven." Susan said again.

"Coven?" I was in another realm with this. "What's that?"

"A coven...," Matie began with another long sigh. She'd been doing a lot of that in the last few days, "Is a group of women ... a group of witches."

"I don't believe this!" Casey was out of her chair and flapping her arms all over the place. "I don't believe this!"

"Where did you hear this?" Matie asked ignoring her niece's outrage as the beginning of some real personal danger started to register.

"I heard this while I was walking the aisles of the supermarket over on Main Street. I overheard two women talking to each other. I recognized one of the ladies from your Church. She was with her two young grandchildren. I didn't recognize the other lady who was doing the talking.

"And I bet the lady talking stopped when she noticed you?" I added.

"Right on." Susan responded making a disgusted face. "Oh, the lady listening ... I think one of the grandchildren was named Jack."

"Jack's grandmother is Jacquelynn Powell," Matie said and then asked, "What did the other woman look like? The one talking to Jacquelynn."

"I just had a fast look, but I'd say mid-fifties, short brown hair, ex-pensive glasses and dressed better than average. She had on a maroon quilted jacket and black pants."

"Did she wear her hair pushed back behind one ear?" Matie asked.

After a moment Susan said. "Why yes. It was pushed back behind her right ear."

"That sounds like Nikki." Matie said.

"The Nikki who left your congregation to join the preacher?" Casey asked.

"One and the same." Matie said not being able to hide her disgust.

"Why the attitude?" Susan asked the Reverend.

"You are a rather astute young woman." Matie said (to which Casey and I smiled at Susan, our trusty smart sanguine leader) "Years ago I was chosen to lead this congregation over Nikki's fiancé."

"Ouch." Susan said to which Casey and I kept looking at our super leader who was ignoring us completely.

"Was the fiancé OK with you being chosen?" Susan asked.

"I think Nikki's fiancé took it better than she did. And Nikki still attended services here once I took the pulpit, but her smiles never went no further than her face."

"Where's her fiancé now?" Casey asked.

"He became the Pastor of a little Church east of Houston, and I've been told that he is rather happy there." Matie said and then added with suspicion in her voice, "But it was Stellie, his sister who told me that."

The room fell silent. Each woman looked at the other.

"I don't know which direction to look at?" Casey said.

"Maybe Stellie or her brother or Nikki is behind all this?" Susan thought out loud.

"Maybe they're all in it together? Even the preacher," I added. I know, I should keep my mouth shut sometimes. Even I knew this was like so far-fetched that I deserved all the 'that's the stupidest thing we've ever heard' looks I was being given.

Casey who was back in her seat working the problem said, "Maybe it's just the new preacher man? It did all start when he dropped into Gening?"

After another few moment of silence Susan said, "O.K. Claire Elizabeth you keep on the tech trail, Casey you keep at the books and the Reverend and I are going to sit down and have a heart to heart about the people that left your Church and went cleaving to this preacher man."

And right on cue the rest of us said in unison, "Cleave?!"

We all laughed, and then I switched the bug back on and we went back on the air with our script for the next ten minutes; for the benefit of the prying ears connected to Matie's house.

We were becoming expert at this double life of ad-libbing. You could say our conversations were almost boring.

Just to keep the ears from being too suspicious we offhandedly mentioned a bit of gossip here or a bit there but we made no fuss or bother over it. Matie kept a running account of the gossip so we didn't repeat any too often. She was definitely Casey's aunt - efficient and organized.

Later that evening Jacquelynn called Matie to tell her what she'd heard in the supermarket. Jacquelynn spent an hour on the phone with Matie discussing how to handle the gossip when it was told to her face … other than doing physical damage to the perpetrator; which Matie was firmly against. (LOL.)

Jacquelynn? Not so much.

43

"So? David asked when we connected again.

"Weren't you watching?" I demanded.

"Had an emergency. Tell me," he said in his non-committal bland government voice.

"Well ... yeah," I said, "it looks like identity theft."

"How sophisticated?" David asked.

"Good enough."

"Good?"

"OK. It would take someone like me to find it."

"That good Huh?" David said more to himself than to me.

"Yes. And that's what's worrying me. This is not big city stuff, or government stuff. It has the feeling like some sort of con game; by an expert I might add. But Casey's aunt is not wealthy, so I'm stuck."

"Have any ideas who's doing it?"

"I tried not to set off any alarms; I don't want the perpetrator to know I'm coming."

"Perpetrator?" David asked kiddingly.

"Creep!"

"Now that's more like the Claire Elizabeth I know." David said and after a moment of silence he added, "I may be able to get you some real forensic creds, like permanent," David offered.

"What will it cost me," I asked.

"Claire Elizabeth, that is such a leading question. If I said give me six months of your time here in Washington what would you say?"

"Come back to Washington! And work for an agency? Are you kidding? Do you think I've lost my mind?"

"Thought so," David sighed, and continued, "just let me keep looking over your shoulder when you go in."

"You're recording everything I'm doing? Aren't you?"

"Need to have notes to read when I don't have an emergency here." he laughed.

"You're the best David Hathaway."

"OK, stop the padding, and let's get back to our hacker, who you say is good. And who has probably stolen at least one identity already, maybe more, and is up to no good."

"I hadn't really thought that far back. But you're right. What if Casey's aunt isn't his first hit? Maybe he's tried this scheme out before and is getting better as he goes along. So much better that it's almost invisible to the naked eye."

"He?"

"It's usually a he," I snapped.

"Unfortunately, that's usually the case."

Getting empty air, David asked into the phone, "Still on the line?"

"I'm here, just thinking."

"About what?"

"Maybe Casey's aunt isn't the target. She's not rich or in line for a big inheritance, unless some unknown benefactor has her in their will.

"The kind of thing that if they die it all goes to her. But, why all the rumors about her health, and the shit about the cake sale money. It just doesn't add up."

"Claire Elizabeth, I think that's an Agatha Christie plot line."

Ignoring him I said, "How about one of the Reverend's parishioners? Gening is the oldest Baptist Church in the state. There are families who've been coming to it for generations; and Casey tells me that some of them are very wealthy. Or maybe, someone is just out to destroy Matie Cooper for some unknown reason, like a vendetta or revenge or they don't like woman leading a church."

"I actually like the rich parishioner thing, but revenge also works for me. I'll see what I can come up with. And Claire …"

"Yes David."

"Be careful."

"Always am."

"Good."

(I didn't tell him that there were times I wasn't careful. Like the time some freak madman held a gun to my head; but I didn't think it was necessary to go into that. Anyway he's a fib, so he probably knows about it already.)

44

"In case you missed any of the highpoints." I continued.

Mia gave me one of her get real looks. I found it rather cute and continued, "First it was all the rumors, then came the cake sale money fiasco and then the unauthorized bank account mess. Which by now your mom was dissecting, one number at a time. And then came the strike out."

"FINALLY! NOW! This is the juicy spart? Right?" Mia exclaimed practically jumping out of her seat.

"Hey girl! A mysterious preacher man, a hidden transmitter ... nasty rumors, covens and the whole spy thing ... is not juicy enough?"

"CLAIRE! The ball out of the park ... please." Mia was doing the hurry up hand thing.

I smiled. Then I took a long slow breathe.

"During the second Sunday service, that was after Susan and I arrived to join your mom, a real tangible crisis was dumped at Matie's doorstep. Or rather, it was leaning against the side of her church.

"The agitated whispering in the back of the Church was immediately followed by what looked like the whole congregation having a panic attack. Parishioners started running outside.

"Yes, I ran out too. Casey and Susan were way up front and Matie was still at the pulpit. Susan maneuvered herself outside quickly (that's how she, Whitney and Casey won races. They found holes and spaces and barreled though). Casey and her aunt followed the crowd going outside.

There we were. In the parking lot. I tell you true. A wide half circle of people, a hundred deep it seemed, surrounding a good looking kid, not even out of his teens, with a needle hanging out of his arm.

He had this surprised look on his face. Like he couldn't believe what was happening to him.

"The Reverend and your mom pushed their way through the crowd until they stopped dead in their tracks when they saw the kid slumped against the side of the church, like he'd been tossed away."

"Oh my god!" The Reverend Matie Cooper cried out. It was Cayteline Farley's brother Malcolm, lying against the church wall. His mother was wailing, pathetically, on her knees, besides her son.

"When Mr. Farley heard Matie's voice he turned on her.

"The man went into a vicious rage, out there in the lot, in front of the whole congregation, accusing Matie of killing his son. He would had attacked her if the police hadn't arrived just then.

"What's with people? Why do they do such mean things. Matie is such a wonderful person. She's like the best. Well mom and dad are the best ... and you're always there when I need something ... and well Grace and Sam are super ... oh shit you're all great! So why the fuck are people so mean and why do they do such awful things?

"I'm great?" I asked rerouting the conversation.

"Of course you are. Who else would put up with my messing up my tech all the time and teaching me stuff and ... well ... being there for me, like now."

"I'm great? Huh."

"Yeah! You're great!"

"So are a lot of people Mia."

"But a lot are creeps.' Mia sighed.

"As Amel'iya would say, 'It's ravbid misogyny and cultural toxicity' that's the trap. It's hard to avoid or not get caught and squashed like a bug.

"Mia - we're women, we're black and we're smart. And like your great aunt, this combo makes life almost impossible in a world where so many men don't like women and so many women haven't been given the chance to know and explore their own worth."

"It's kind of a really messed up world though if people can do evil to my great aunt."

"Yeah, but your great aunt had a rescue team. And you have a whole squad. You are not alone. Just remember that."

"I guess I'm one of the lucky ones." Mia said and jack rabbited out of her chair to hug me.

So I let her. What else could I do. She's my godchild after all.

(I hadn't told Mia that little did I know until two days after this ghastly event that the coroner was looking at Malcolm's death (almost immediately as it turned out) with suspicion; and then so was the Chief of Police.)

Settling back down Mia said, "You're not making this up? Are you? A needle hanging out of his arm? Was the kid really dead?" Mia was a bit skeptical by this turn of events.

"No my little peach muffin, a kid overdosed outside the church."

"Holy Crap!"

"Exactly."

45

"**A**nd!" Mia insisted.

"And ... that day did not end well."

"First: A doctor had to declare that Malcolm Farley was dead. Then the place was tapped off and all sorts of law enforcement were on the scene. Everyone was forced back into the church to give their names and where they were sitting and did they know Malcom Farley and when was the last time they saw him. And all sorts of stuff like that.

"The people who had parked on the street were allowed to leave first. But the people in the lot were grilled some more. Like what time they arrived, where exactly did they park, what did they see and stuff like that.

Detective Michaels had a board brought over from the police station and two officers were filling in all the blanks as people went to their cars.

"Then: You great aunt was sent home. Casey by her side. Then the chief showed up and the questions began again.

Susan had made a fast look around the parking lot, side and back, while the congregation was swarming around the dead body. She hurried back to us and barked out orders. She was going to find the preacher but wound up following Jaamika to the preacher's office. Ostensibly to inform him about what was going on. But he wasn't at the Church office. Jaamika tried his apartment, but he wasn't there either.

Susan then went searching around town, but the preacher was in the wind. I didn't have any better luck locating Michelle. I did find Nikki, but that was like after two hours of running all over town.

46

Once inside the house, the chief sat down across from the Reverend and said, "Reverend Cooper," making sure he had Matie's full attention.

He began, "You're telling me that this kid ..."

"Malcolm Farley!" Matie said very deliberately staring hard at the chief. She wasn't going to let him get away with stripping Malcolm's personhood away..

"'You're telling me that ... Malcolm Farley," the chief said, "was up against your Church wall ... a drug addict who you were trying to help, and a person you were the last one to actually see alive ... just happened to die right there against the side of "Your" church? And you know nothing about it?"

"That's exactly what I'm telling you."

"That's pretty hard to swallow."

"Then I'll get you a glass of water Chief Wojick." Matie said in exasperation.

Before the chief could respond Casey said, "Malcolm didn't kill himself if that's what you're thinking."

"And you know this how young lady?"

"Because he was doing great. My aunt told you that! Like a dozen times the first time you questioned her at the church. And my name is Casey."

"Now. I know you're all upset bu... ."

Matie jackknifed out of her seat and stood there glowering down at the chief with her hands on her hips.

She was almost shouting when she said, "I will tell you again, and for the last time, that young man did rehab, he lived in great community house, he had a job and he's been clean for months."

"We're checking on that Ms. Casey." the detective said in a calm reassuring voice that took the wind out of Casery's sails. "But what I want to know is why a packet of an illegal substance was found in your church office, in the back of your bottom drawer?"

With that bombshell the room went dead silent.

Matie touched her Csey's arm.

Casey sat down before she said something she would regret.

Matie took a moment to collect her thoughts before she spoke. It may have been a new millennium but she was a black woman mixing with the chief; a white man. The wind would not be blowing in her favor.

Just before Matie started to answer the chief, Casey stopped the interview by standing up again, and saying, "I'll walk you to the door Chief."

To our amazement he stood up.

Casey walked the chief and his detective out to the front gate where she said, "My aunt had nothing to do with Malcolm's death. If there was some illegal substance in her desk it was planted there. Furthermore … I don't care if she was the last person to see Malcolm or the fiftieth. And if you're interested at all, someone is trying to hurt my aunt."

The young detective, black and new to the force, immediately asked, "Has she been threatened?" The chief looked surprised, first at Casey and then at his detective.

"Not specifically." Casey offered, "just a lot of nasty rumors, and missing money that wasn't missing; and lots of gossip going around that's all untrue. And now a kid she was helping winds up dead against the church she leads."

The detective looked at the chief, who had a scowl plastered on his face.

He turned back to the two women quickly saying, "Maybe you and your aunt should come into the station tomorrow and tell us about what you think is going on."

"We'd be glad to!" Casey said belligerently knowing that the chief wouldn't believe that her aunt was in any real danger. But maybe the detective might?

Matie was a nervous wreck. "They think I had something to do with Malcolm's death … how could this happen? it feels like everything's falling apart. And how did they find anything illegal in my desk?"

Casey pulled her aunt close in a hug and whispered in her ear. "It's all right aunt Matie. You're right. That boy was pulling himself up. I know you're worried but we're going to figure this out."

"But drugs? In my desk? How could that happen?" Matie moaned.

By this point Susan and I had come back to hear Casey trying to comfort her aunt and heard Matie talking about drugs in her desk.

Casey looked over at us.

Susan took notice. Her face went back into her thinking hard mode. I gave Casey a worried look. Matie was now crying against Casey's shoulder.

Matie's world had taken a deep dive into the fiery pit of hell and the three of us didn't quite know exactly how we were going to put out the fire. Yet.

47

Michelle quietly joined the small crowd that was still mingling at the end of the block, watching and whispering.

The body of Malcom Farley had been removed and taken to the morgue. Crime scene tape was still up. The police were going house to house and most of the congregation had left. Michelle stood at her window watching and listening.

She smiled as she thought - maybe Matie'd even be arrested? Maybe she'd even go to jail? Everyone's going to think she's connected with the kid's death. Especially since it looks like he chose to overdose right there against the church wall. That'll finish her off for good.

48

Early the next morning Matie and Casey arrived at the police station looking a bit zombied. Both had slept fitfully.

Detective Michaels and Chief Wojick were waiting for them. Neither man was in a good mood.

Casey and her aunt were offered seats which they accepted.

They were offered coffee which they declined.

The Chief sat behind his desk scrutinizing the two women with his flat hard cop face.

Casey was glad they weren't put into an interrogation room like she'd seen on some TV shows. Being in a room with windows made her feel a lot calmer.

It was Casey and her aunt's turn to tell them what was had been happening to warrant worrying the Reverend.

They chronologically listed the gossip and events that had been going on.

Chief Wojick asked, "Why didn't you come and tell us all this before?"

Casey looked at her aunt. Something had changed since yesterday. The chief was being, maybe not cordial but definitely not antagonistic.

"What was there to tell? What could you do. No one was breaking the law."

"Well Reverend, the law's been broken now."

Matie looked alarmed and reached for Casey's hand.

The chief closely watched the reverend's reaction for tell-tale signs of obfuscation as he said, "We have a murder on our hands."

Matie gasped and Casey jumped up out of her seat. She was furious at herself for thinking this white man was going to be …. going to be …. what? Maybe a good cop?

"Ladies! Neither of you are suspects! O.K.?" He turned to his detective who gave an imperceptive nod of agreement and said, "Michaels get some water for these ladies."

"Murder!" Casey exclaimed as she fell back into her seat. Matie was in shock.

He gave them a minute to collect themselves while Casey made her aunt drink some water.

"Yes, murder. I've known you for a long time Reverend. We sometimes have a difference of opinions, many more than just some differences I will concede, but I wouldn't think you had any enemies. Not the murdering kind. But it's looking like you might have some and if this kid's … sorry … Malcolm's death is linked to whoever is against you, then we need to tread careful here."

The women were speechless. And frightened.

"First, we usually don't talk about the case, but there is something very wrong here about the boy's death, and I would like you to keep any information I am willing to share with both of you absolutely quiet. Is that acceptable?"

"Yes." Casey squeaked while her aunt shook her head. She was unable to find her voice.

"The tube we found in your drawer, filled with an illegal substance, had been wiped clean. Plus, I'm being told, it's a heroine combination that hasn't been on the streets for over twenty years. And it appears as though some of this same stuff was used on Malcolm. We don't know how or why, but we will find out.

At the moment forensics is looking into tagging this old drug to cold cases, which is all going to bust my yearly budget, but we're going to do it."

Casey and Matie's eyes were bulging by now. The chief wondered for a moment if they were in shock?

"Reverend? Casey? are you both all right? Do you want to take a few minutes to collect yourselves?"

"No!" Came the response in unison from the two women.

"O.K.," the chief said. He took a few seconds to set his words in the right order and continued, "not only do you have an alibi, Reverend, for the time of death; but first appearances suggest someone is setting you up."

The chief then sat back in his chair in a less confrontational manner.

Matie kept staring, eyes wide and stunned.

Ahh Casey thought so that was why he'd put on a nice face.

"An alibi. Like a whole congregation!" Casey was mad as she accused him of … she didn't know what … .

He noted the confrontational manner in the young woman's manner.

"Yes, as a matter of fact. A whole congregation." He conceded with a nod.

He turned back to Matie. "What I want to know is when did all these rumors start?"

Matie took a moment to calm herself. "About the time preacher Charmeur arrived in town."

"Do you know him?"

"Met him once, don't want to do that again."

Casey noticed her aunt didn't offer any information on Charmeur. They were learning more and more about him every day and none of it was good. But neither Matie nor her niece were going to give him this little piece of information. Not yet anyway.

"That's pretty strong words for a Reverend."

"Maybe not strong enough Chief Wojick."

After taking note that he was now Chief Wojick, with a very big capital C, he decided to watch his step. The mayor and his wife had a friendly relationship with the Reverend, going back a decade or more. He didn't want to make waves right now, especially with a murder to solve.

"Any enemies you might have?" Detective Michaels asked.

"I wouldn't think so, but it seems that I have some."

Before Matie and Casey came back to the rectory, after their session with the police, a tall man, slightly nervous, came into the office looking for Matie.

49

"Excuse me," he said, "I'm Nathanial Powell. Jacquelynn's husband. Is the Reverend here?"

"I'm sorry, the Reverend is still at the police station," Susan responded; ticking off the gentleman's attributes: Late thirties, early forties, perfectly tailored, European shoes, high end eyeglasses, married, well-spoken, tall, with a cultured look about him and strong handsome black features.

"You're friends of the Reverend's niece - I presume?" He said looking questioningly at the two women in front of him.

"Yes we are Susan answered. Can we help you?"

"Is the Reverend here?"

"Not at the moment." Susan said.

"Well ... I don't' know what's going on here, but this whole thing - about all these rumors - and now blaming Matie for Malcolm dyeing on the side of the church is totally outrageous.

"I don't know what's going on but I'm here to help the Reverend in any way I can, and the whole Church board is with me."

"Thank you so much Mr. Powell. I'll tell the Reverend what you said and I'm sure she'll be calling you as soon as she can." I said.

His voice softened up as he said, "I've talked to the Reverend about the rumors when I first heard about them. They were all absurd. Especially this last one that Nikki told my wife. But if there's one thing I'm certain of now, it's that someone has it in for our Reverend. I see this kind of back stabbing bullshit in business ... I just never expected to see it in my own Church."

"We also think the same way Mr. Powell. But we need to get to the bottom of this before it really gets out of hand. We just don't know yet what we are dealing with." I said.

"And you are friends of the Referend's neice?" Mr. Powell asked again.

"Yes, Mr. Powell, we ae friends of Casey, the Reverend's niece," Susan answered, "from Kerry, Ohio."

Mr. Powell mulled this information over for a moment and then asked, "Did both of you come because of these rumors?"

"Yes we did Mr. Powell. And we've been looking into them." Susan said.

"And what have you found?" He looked at Susan and then at me.

"Too many threads to say for sure." I said, in what I hoped was a non-committal response.

Mr. Powell looked from Susan to me and back again before he said, "Please have Reverend Cooper call me.

"We'll be sure to let her know." Susan said.

When Mr. Powell left, I looked at Susan and half-questioningly said, "He seems like a nice guy ... doesn't he?"

Susan instantly morphed into her gold medal 'I'm woman voice' and declared:

"NO ONE'S A NICE GUY UNTIL I SAY HE'S A NICE GUY! Got it?!"

"Got it." I squeaked.

"That evening, after your great aunt dragged herself upstairs to her bedroom and still dressed, passed out from fatigue, Susan, your mom and I went outside into Matie's backyard,

"We stood outside, in the dark, in a closed circle. By then I didn't know if whoever was mining the house, and vestry, for information might have some long distance audio surveillance on us."

Mia looked at me like I'd gone loopy.

"I know! I know! But I was paranoid by that time."

"O.K. I understand. So what did you do?"

"Susan took the lead. Remember she was in her five star woman general mode by then. "There's a dead kid in the morgue right now and we need more help."

She looked at me, I looked at your mom and your mom looked at Susan who then told us, "I know she has this infernal deadline and she has to watch that gadget you are working on Claire, but I'm calling Amel'iya. We need her." She said and waited to see if there was any decent.

I looked at Casey and Casey looked at Susan and Susan looked at the two of us, and hearing no decent she nodded and said, "Claire give me that special phone thingy of yours or do you still have it Cas?"

"Susan actually said 'phone thingy'. You must be making that up." Mia laughed.

"I swear on your little wedge shoes, that's what she said."

"So?" Mia said rolling her teenage eyes.

"So I gave her the phone thingy. I'd taken it back from your mom.

"Susan called Amel'iya and told her what was going on. After she hung up we asked her what Amel'iya said, even though your mom and I knew exactly what was going to happen."

"She's walking out the door to get the bikemobile and is headed our way as we speak."

"O.K. that I don't believe. What? A five minute call and she's packed and on the road? And what's a bikemobile?" Mia gave me the 'you're lying squint' she'd seem to have perfected.

"You don't know Amel'iya. That's usual for her. She's like some wonder woman or something. Strange sometimes, but she knows stuff and when she and Susan go on the hunt or arrange stuff they are like a navy seal team. Terrifying. No one gets in their way."

"You're exaggerating. Susan? The Susan I know?"

"Oh! If you only knew my little sparrow. The two of them have always been on the same wave length when it comes to action. The rest of us find it a bit creepy, but whenever there was trouble there was

Amel'iya and Susan. They'd get us out of trouble or push us where we needed to go."

"It must have been pretty awful when she …..?"Mia's voice trailed off as I gave her a look that stopped her from venturing into Amel'iya traitorous actions.

"Sorry." She squeeked.

"Where was I?" I said with clenched teeth.

"Going into the kitchen for some chamomile tea."

"You've read my mind cutie." I said getting up and squeezing her shoulder a little so she didn't think I was mad or anything.

"Hey! What's a bikemobile?" Mia said as she jumped up to follow me.

"Competitions. Travel. Take bikes and accessories." I hinted.

50

Nikki watched from behind her window as Nathanial Powell left the church. He held a good deal of power in the church, but his father, Del Powell, was the financial pocket that spilled out the money to keep the church going. When senior Powell saw the photographs she had it would be the end of Matie Cooper.

The photographs were safely tucked away. This dead kid put a wrench in her own plans. But maybe it would still work out. She thought.

When things quieted down a bit, she would go to Matie Cooper and tell her to get out of town or she would show her photographs to old Mr. Powell.

The new preacher man had asked her about the old man. Strange she thought at the time.

He'd asked if the old man liked Reverend Cooper; in a way that suggested he already knew that Del Powell didn't very much like a woman preaching in his church. She was sure that Mr. Del Powell detested the Reverend Dr. Matie Cooper.

He'd believe the worst that the pictures insinuated. That she was also sure of.

Maybe ... maybe, she thought, she might spread another rumor.

Matie was a good-looking woman and maybe the younger Powell was a man-whore cheater like his old man. It wasn't too far-fetched, she told herself.

There were a lot of people she knew who would believe it.

Nathanial Powell's old father would believe it. He'd believe he picture of his son in the arms of Matie Cooper; because this is what men did with women, any woman, according to the old man's bible.

But old man Powell didn't like scandal. Of any kind.

He'd even begrudgingly supported the appointment of the Reverend Dr. Cooper in order to avoid any scandal while continuing to hold his position as the head patriarch of the church.

He'd figured she wouldn't last a month. But, here she still was.

Nikki, staring at the church with bitterness flooding her whole being, was going to put her money on Dell Powell's total dislike of the Cooper woman being stronger than a bit of bad publicity.

In fact, he'd throw his son under the proverbial bus to get rid of Cooper. That's the kind of man he was. She thought.

(What the pictures didn't say was that Nathanial and Jacquely's son had been in a comma for weeks after a car accident. The kid recovered all right, but Nikki had pictures of the kid's father in the arms of the Reverend Dr. Matie Cooper.

Nathanial Powell had come to pray for his son and wound up weeping in Cooper's arms. The photos didn't show the tears, only the clinging.)

Nikki Brown had been the new preacher man's first recruit.

When she first saw him, she thought he looked a lot like her ex-fiancée, Stellie's brother. The one who left town when the Reverend Dr. Matie Cooper took the pulpit at Springrock. The one who left her behind.

51

The day Susan and Casey showed up at the mission storefront to check him out, the Preacher was talking about pencils and notebooks for the little children of a distant village in the heart of the Amazon jungle. He talked mightily about the children who wanted to learn to read and write, but who had nothing to practice with.

After the service, Susan and Casey made the rounds asking off handedly about the preacher. His congregants were very eager to fill them in.

The women received a grandiose sanitized version of the life and times of Preacher Charmeur, with fantastical embellishments.

Afterwards they dropped a five dollar bill in the donation box and were profusely thanked by the young man at the door, dressed in classic 1950's Jehovah witness attire and matching haircut.

Casey and Susan weren't told, probably because no one knew, that the Preacher Daniel Charmeur, had driven unseen into town - behind the wheel of a green four door Chrysler; sporting out of town plates. A car he parked in a rented garage space four blocks away.

When first seen, he was walking along Main Street looking into shop windows.

He was a tall man of ethereal features wearing dark clothes.

Every Sunday, after his uneventful relocation to Gening, he would show up at one of the Churches in town. He'd sit quietly in the back until hymn time.

Then his voice could be heard bouncing from wall to wall. He had a fine voice and every black parishioner became familiar with his presence.

After Nikki Brown and Stellie Nelson were recruited, there was Jaamika Jones – also from Springrock Baptist, and then DeShawn Farley, who attended the Episcopal Church (he was a second cousin to Mr. Farley, Cayteline's father who attended the Springrock Baptist Church). And then came J.D,. Pace Betts and her brother Jordon. They were plucked out of the Springrock Baptist Church. He made a brief stop at the Catholic Church and tagged May Adams and her sister Spring - and it went on like this - back and forth, from one house of worship to the next and then back again, for five months until the preacher had his fifty soft souls.

He had an experts eye.

He raided almost every Church in Gening, but mostly he took from Springrock.

And he played them all like a world class pianist.

"The lit'tle child'drn go to sleep hun'gry," Preacher Charmeur began … bellowing each syllable … speaking slowly … making sure every part of every word he uttered had the proper effect he was looking for.

When the heads of the parishioners who had joined his Church of Mercy started nodding in understanding he continued; once again slowly rolling every word out to its full length. "They need mon'ey … YES mon'ey good people of Gening… for little seeds … so … their vill'age, a place of pov … er … ty, will have food to eat. They need these little seeds … from god … in order to keep the spec'tar of star'vay'tion … and wild vicious an'e'mals … from the doors of the little … star'ving … chil'drn."

All the parishioners knew what he was talking about. They had all seen the pictures of the village, and the malnourished dark-skinned children that were in the Mercy Mission book. A thick bound book kept on the table by the back wall, by the exit, by the donation box.

By the time he was half way through, his audience sat rapt at attention. For there were always, snakes, crocodiles and obstacles in his Indiana Jones narratives. It was a world he made up in his head and delivered with the best storytelling technique of a true con artist.

No one in his hand-picked audience (wherever he had set up shop) could tell the difference between fantasy and reality. This is why they were chosen.

Not one of them had ever been to any village, in any far-off country … like the ones the preacher man talked about. And none of them ever expected or wanted to go see one.

They were all armchair missionaries.

For their pennies and dollars, Preacher Charmeur gave them what they craved. Gratitude, self-worth and something of world importance to be a part of.

He planted the seeds first. Delivering them came next. And then water to make them grown came third.

"I tell you broth'ers and sis'tas … these poor … down trod'den women … walk two and a half miles, yes I said two and a half miles, over dry hard land … and then two and a half hours back, to bring war'ta, clean fresh war'ta home in jugs. Hev'ee jugs … that they carry … on their heads. Yes! On their heads I say.

Good people of Gening! These down trod'den people, their well dried up …. and here we sit in our com'for'table homes … with god's good clean war'ta running out of our taps … but these poor people … have noth'in. Not even the few dollars to dig a new well … for the little seeds to grow."

When the heads started nodding - understanding the plight of these poor woman - he continued, "And all they need … is … a new well. Noth'in fan'cee. No artisan war'ta for these poor people. Just good clean war'ta. To drink … and for the little seeds to grow."

Congregants swayed and nodded to his song. One lucrative Mercy Mission project after another.

His flair for dramatic recitation was augmented each week with large brightly colored visuals. Preacher Charmeur would show his congregation the letters and pictures of what they had accomplished in far off places, and the smiling faces and hands of the people there who waved their hands in greetings to the people who were so generous as to help them.

"Look here! God lov'in people of Gening." The Preacher would call out in his slow way of giving every word the importance of royalty. "Look at what good you have done. Look at the good works you are doing," he said as he held up another book, waiting for the effect and then placing it down on the pulpit.

"But now I hear of another village ... in need ... in another land ... where a drought, yes a Bibical drought ... ravaged their fields ... brought DOWN their homes ... and their lives! Good people of Gening, let's bring another act of mercy to these poor suffer'in people."

And so, the donation box kept being filled and his congregation went forth and brought in small donations from friends, family and neighbors.

The Preacher was firm about everyone giving what they could and pressuring no one for more than they could afford. A quarter was looked on as godly as a dollar. So, the quarters and dollars came in on a regular basis.

52

"There is a Daniel Charmeur. He does exist. But, he's an 80-year-old man who I'm told lives with the whole Charmeur clan in an idyllic little village in the Ozarks." David Hathaway told Claire Elisabeth.

"So, the guy here's a fake. Why doesn't that surprise me?" I said in my most sarcastic voice.

Ignoring my reaction, which he always does, he said, "But, here's the interesting part. The license plate on his car is registered to a Claudaye Brownne who lives in Nebraska."

"And?" I prompted.

"And, Claudaye Brownne sold her Chrysler with its plates to her preacher three years ago. And she told my agent that she got a very fair price for it too."

"Three years? But the car and plates are up to date."

Now there's the other interesting part of this puzzle. Ms. Brownne swore that the DMV in her state stopped sending her renewals as soon as she sold the car. She was most emphatic about that I've been told."

"So, her preacher may be our preacher, and if he is, then he's able to get into government files and alter them."

"That's what it looks like to us. And that's sophisticated hacking. So now it's officially in my court."

"Was your agent able to find out anything about our Flim-Flam man?"

"I always like your turn of phrase Claire. So let me tell you that I sent out one of my best, and, she was able to find out that a professor over at the university in Ms. Brownne's town was involved in some scandal. Ms. Brownne remembers the incident because the preacher left town soon after."

"And." I said because David had stopped for effect.

"And – and it seemed he was headed out to Africa to do gods work hands-on. And if you wonder about the car Ms. Stockton? He was going to drive it to New York and sell it there to help with his air fare to the dark continent."

"She actually said dark continent?"

"Those were the exact words out of the god-fearing woman's mouth."

"Shit. I'm getting a wave length here about this guy, like maybe he's going around cherry-picking gullible bible-blind congregants, like some of the people we saw here at his service. People who are needy, ignorant and whatever else you want to tag them with."

"I'm still working on the list you provided, but for now, the bad news. And that's about the thread you found in the bank's records. We've followed it … ."

"And? … Go on!"

"It leads to a thousand different accounts all over the world. All inconsequential amounts were transferred, but it all comes from Matie Cooper's account."

"Shit! I thought it might be that." I did not like the ramifications of a scenario like this. "So … I need to find a back door… and go in after the source? And if I do that, I'll tip him or whomever off and then they run for cover, vanish, go puff into the cosmos."

"Let's try the catch not vanish way. I prefer it that way. I have a net out at the moment. Let's see what I can catch." David said and hung up.

53

When he called back, David Hathaway stated without any preamble, "The good news is that it looks like we found a pattern. Granted, the net I threw was a very wide one, so the pattern is sketchy; but it pulled in a disgraced professor in Nebraska plus two clergy, who, from all accounts, swear they are innocent. As it happens, the Professor was able to clear herself but she lost her position, her reputation and is in the courts suing everyone, and rightly so. "

"And the clergy? Were they woman too?" I asked but kind of assumed I knew what the answer would be.

"Yes, as a matter of fact. One was a reverend and the other two were pastors. What it's shaping up to look like is that three women were set up as patsies to take the fall for a digital raid. One was a wealthy donor to the university and the other two were wealthy parishioners. And, each of the three women wound up being the fall guy?"

"What's the feminine for fall guy?" I asked in my most innocent voice

"I'm not going there Claire."

"Smart."

"That's why they pay me the big bucks." David said amused."

"Let me get this straight … you now have three names and no substance on this preacher?"

"As far as the preacher goes, we could be looking at more than one person, but I'm going the easy way first and assume it's one guy. Your guy. We'll know soon enough. We've started showing the photos you sent of "your" preacher, as we speak. My agent's gone back to Nebraska to Ms. Brownne, and then she's going to the Professors, and then she has to run down the reverend and the pastors to show them the pictures and see if we can ID your preacher … and connect the dots. Right now, your preacher man only has one foot in the frame, so I need to button that down first. When I'm sure it's him, we'll set him up and take him down."

"And to do that either I need to find a way to trap him or you need to find a way. I'm volunteering for the digital leg work. And no! I'm not coming to Washington to use the big bad machine."

"I am told if you call it a machine, there could be bloodshed."

"Oh, give me a break." I shot back.

"Seriously, I'm thinking that if these other cons were test runs or he was perfecting his scheme, for a big hit, you might look for a very wealthy person connected with the Reverend. The three cases we caught in our web were larceny, but not extravagant. One was for a hundred thousand plus change. Another one for a hundred and seventy-five and the third for two hundred thousand.

David paused before adding, "If it's the same person, doing the same con, he's slowly moving on up the ladder."

"If he goes for two hundred thousand this time … ."

"How about a few million?" David interrupted. "I've got a feeling."

"You're kidding! Come on David. A FEW MILLION!?"

"There's always a big jump to any con."

"BUT … a few million!?"

"Would you consider that extravagant?" David asked.

"That would do it."

"As soon as we decide that this person is your preacher, we can start to connect the dots and see what his game plan is. It would help if Casey could give up some specifics."

"I've been turning digital into reams of paper for her. She's a hound on the scent. thinks she's found a thread. And… she's pulling on it at this very moment. As soon as she finds the trail you'll know.

"I keep forgetting that you're not city."

"You're funny alphabet man."

"Seriously, if you can lock down this Charmeur person and attach him solidly to the Reverend that would help."

"If only," I said and added, "He has a cell. You might want to see if he made any calls to the three places involved. From people who might still be looking out for his interests.

"I have a follower here in Gening, who if asked, would be his look-out in a hot second Susan says the people in his congregation are not exactly groupies, but something akin to that state of mind."

"Oh joy. And do they come at us with guns if we arrest him on main street?" David asked actually dreading a scenario like that.

"I'll ask Susan to work on that. She can categorize people better than anyone I know. That is except Amel'iya."

"Do I gather that Ms. Jackson's on her way to enjoy the wonders of nature in the Hudson 'Valley?" David asked.

"Of course she's on her way here. By the end of this all eight of us might be here.

"But, for the next few hours, give or take a minute or two, it'll just be the three of us. Susan will spy, gather and correlate and Casey and I will stay at the numbers and accounts. She may figure all this out in the next five minutes for all I know. As I just mentioned she thinks she may have found the ghoul's string that we can pull on."

"If she does, you will inform me? Immediately? Right?" David said; making sure I hadn't forgotten, in like the last two seconds, that he was my important link to the Washington eye in the sky.

"As I said, you'll be the first. Actually David, it's my goal to always give you scum like this to do with as you please. But just remember, it's important that Casey's aunt, or anyone in her congregation, doesn't get the blow-back or hurt from what we do."

"Will do our best. But shit goes sideways sometimes Claire."

"Yeah I know." I was not happy at this exact moment.

"Does she need help?" David slide the question in while I wasn't looking.

"NO!" I knew where he was going with this. He's always dangling bait in front of me. (I may need what he's offering, but I need to be real careful if it comes to that.)

"Ms. Stockton?"

"O.K., I'll ask her."

"Do that … and I have people headed to you. Be nice to them."

"I always play nice in the sandbox. It's always the other fuckin bastards who start throwing sand."

"Claire Elizabeth Stockton…"

"Yes David?"

"Nothing! Good bye."

"Bye David," I said in clean language.

(I've used much stronger and smellier language around him in the past.)

(Hey! Poverty speaks a different language where I came from. Rough, hard and ugly. Yeah, I've cleaned it up. I even enunciate my words real good so func'in dizzards in idiot-land, who pay me lots of Benjamins, understand what the fuck I'm telling them.)

That night I found the hack.

Same signature.

Hackers have a way of writing and placing code that's like a fingerprint.

I found the same person who'd invaded Matie's bank account. They'd done a pretty decent job of erasing their trail. (Not good enough that I couldn't get through their invisibility cloak, but what they did shouldn't be possible for your average hacker or even techwiz.)

David agreed with me when I notified him.

He didn't like the implication for the alphabet security agencies in his neck of the woods.

"Can you get any closer, unseen?" David asked me.

"Not with what I'm working with. You know that. But you can do it on your end!"

"I'll let you use …." He started.

"I'm not going to Washington! And, I'm not going near that machine of yours."

David sighed.

He then said, "We have a place down in the city where I can connect you with better access then what you're working with."

"New York City! Are you kidding!"

"I'll set it up and have a car waiting for you tomorrow, let's say around six in the morning." David said and hung up.

And then, Casey, bless her little mathematical heart, found another person (this time tied to Springrock) who played a part in this ongoing nightmare.

54

At supper that evening Casey sat at the kitchen table with an ice-cold cucumber pack over both her eyes.

"She's not going blind, is she?" I asked Susan as I shoved in another mouthful of the most delicious meat stew I've ever eaten.

"No. Just cross-eyed," Susan responded.

Matie was shoveling some of the stew onto a fork and handed it to Casey.

"I'd really appreciate it if you two didn't talk over my head like I wasn't in the room," Casey complained, "by the way I think I've found who's being targeted and it's actually not my aunt, but her identity is being used according to what you've found out Claire." And then she put the contents of the fork into her mouth and chewed.

"Who?" Matie, Susan and I asked all at once, "and how?"

"Ah! So now they talk to me," Casey said after swallowing.

"Cas!" Susan said in her most authoritarian supreme leader voice.

With one hand Casey pulled the right side of the icepack off that eye and looked at her aunt, "Sorry aunt Matie but I think it's that nice older man I saw at the board meeting that first night I came.

"On my goodness. You don't mean Mr. Powell? Jacquelynn's father-in-law? He's such a good man, worked hard all his life, and he happens to be one of our biggest supporters," Matie said, slumping a bit in her chair.

"Reverend?" Susan asked.

"I'm sorry. All this just seems so unreal. Like some big bad awful dream."

"Reverend?" Susan asked again.

"Yes Susan."

"What can you tell us about Mr. Powell?"

Matie sat up, looked around the table and nodded her head. "Del Powell worked his way through school, and his mother worked her fingers to the bone to see that he got the education she never had.

"The day he received a scholarship to Harvard, for their master's program, was the proudest day of his mother's life I've been told. Del doesn't talk much about her but Jacquelynn, his daughter-in-law, did tell me that Del's mother died just before he got his PhD.

"After that he was snatched up by IBM where he worked his way up as project manager, which wasn't easy, what with him being a black man. And then he went into the hedge fund business where he had more mobility and opportunities.

"And yes, he made a fortune.

"He's finally going to retire this year. Oh, and he likes being active on the board.

"Del, and a few other men in the church, would like me to only stick to ole'time religion … a bit of hellfire and brimstone, gospels and the resurrection kind of sermons. It's been a running battle between us for years.

Dell Powell is what I would call a hard man.

"Now his son, Nathanial, on the other hand, is a kind man who has a sort of love hate relationship with his dad.

"And … Del's daughter-in-law Jacquelynn, Nathanial's wife, is one of my best friends!"

And then the room went quiet as everyone became lost in their thoughts. After a few more mouthfuls, handed over by her aunt, while she continued to hold the icepack in place, she popped up and said, "Claire Elizabeth I need to go treasure hunting again. Do you think you can get back into the bank's records?"

The silence lasted so long that Casey finally peeked out from behind the pack to find that I was staring at her with the are-you-kidding-me look. I was still hunting, but bank records again? I did have creds, and I was going into the city in the morning, but I'm quite sure David did not mean I could go surfing and snooping for what Casey was asking for.

"OK! OK." Casey surrendered and went behind her cold eye-pack again.

"You need ALL of old man Powell's information, don't you?" I just surrendered and skipped to the end.

What I'd been doing was every which way illegal, somewhat, but David knew what I was doing. Right? And David hadn't explicitly told me to stop looking far afield. He hadn't sent the feds knocking on our door with a warrant for my arrest, and I WAS headed to the satellite big machine in the city tomorrow – so I figured that I was still good to go. Right?

"If we want to catch that piss preacher, or whomever is doing this, I need the info, and then I can give you and your secret agent man a plan." Casey barked. She was tired. Casey never barks. Growls sometimes, but never barks.

With those words Susan reached over and patted Matie's hand in reassurance. Matie was sitting there with an empty fork in the air. Someone needed to tell her to breathe.

"Actually, it looks like I'll probably be able to get you the info you need," I said pulling an edge of the pack away to look into one red eye."

Registering Susan's reaction and Matie's eyes going wide I said, "I did some work for the government, once, and they granted me three wishes."

Matie was befuddled and looked at Susan who said, "It's OK Reverend, not to worry."

"As I was saying, I have three wishes and I called in one wish (I didn't tell them everything of course) - and – it kind of looks like we've found three other woman - who were used, probably by the preacher, to run a swindle on a third party."

"I knew it! A shell game." Casey said pulling the pack from her eyes; which though still a bit red, did look a lot better.

"But how can anyone just go steal money and no one knows who it was or rather that it wasn't the person who was blamed?" Matie asked confused.

"Identity Theft aunt Matie." Casey said.

"What?"

"Someone steals your name, address, social security number, driver's license, access codes, password – well everything about you that can digitally identify you. And then he sets up a parallel you. Like a shadow.

"But how?" Matie asked again.

"Through the ether Reverend. Through the one and zero highway in the sky," I offered.

"Through the internet?" Matie asked.

"Actually, through the programs on various computers. The internet is just the phone line."

"I need to tell Mr. Powell immediately. I can't have him harmed."

"No!" We all said as once.

"Now listen here ladies. It's one thing if I have to protect myself, or take a punch or two, but it's totally another thing, all together, to stand by, and let someone harm or ruin another person."

"No one is going to harm anyone." Casey said, "isn't that right Claire Elizabeth? Susan?"

"We're going to stop whoever is doing this. And! We need to keep this all right here for the moment. But we will stop the bad guys. That's a given." I assured Matie.

"And I'm off to the city in the morning to play with a big computer. Should have a lot of answers by lunch time."

Susan looked at me and then at Casey, and then smiled and said, "You're going off the track and Amel'iya's crossing the river as we speak. What can go wrong?"

Matie was still holding her fork in mid-air. "City? Computer?"

Casey took off the ice pack putting it on the table. She took the fork out of her aunt's hand and put her other hand around her aunt's shoulder. Matie turned her head to look at her niece and gave her a weak half smile, more like a grimace.

55

"When Susan told Casey and me she was calling in Amel'iya to help, we weren't surprise."

Mia's eye flew wide open, "So, Amel'iya to the rescue?"

"In a way, yes. Susan and Amel'iya had …. I guess you could say they were kind of cut from the same cloth type. That's the way Grace explains it.

"It's not like they they're connected at the hip or anything like that, but they both have this weird wave they'd get on, and automatically, they'd just go in the same direction.

"Like something on the edge of devious and conspiratorial. Not with each other, but in general; like they face the world in the same way. And they understand each other without saying more than two words.

"No, none of us understand it. Yes, it's bizarre." I said to the teenager giving me one of her 'are you for real' looks.

After which she said, "And? And!" Mia had to give me a prompt. I was going off-topic again.

"And! Susan and Amelia did more that first day they worked together then we had done in the time we were there. They figured out who was naughty and who was nice

"Claire! You've got to be kidding! Naughty or Nice?"

"O.K. Here goes. When I got back from the city and we were all congregated out back; by the way your great-aunt has a great garden. Amel'iya was going to say something crude, rude or do some curse-talkin her report about what she'd found; but Susan stopped her with the naughty or nice thing. Amelia just gave Susan one of her squints."

Mia was laughing so hard now I had to stop and let her get herself under control. "Why?" Was all she could get out.

"God damn it Mia, Matie Cooper is a Reverend. You can't just blurt out curse-language. Don't look at me like that! That's what we thought then."

"My great aunt has curses even I haven't heard." Mia exclaimed with all the hand waving movements that go along with that statement.

"Well, we found that out later on, now didn't we! But when it all started we though she was a nice clean mouthed lady. I mean we hadn't heard any bad language out of her mouth."

"OK, so Amel'iya came and ...?"

"And she and Susan connected all the rumors with the instigators and put the preacher into .... but I'm getting ahead of myself.

55

Amel'iya came flying into town in Susan and Casey's Chevy van with their equipment plus their two practice bikes strapped to the inside wall.

Susan had originally wanted us to drive the van straight through to New York, but we had to get to Casey fast, so she left the Chevy with Amel'iya.

Amel'iya wanted wheels in Gening, and Susan wanted the bikes, so van, bikes and Amel'iya came as a package.

"She probably didn't even stop to .... Well, she probably just drove straight through," Susan said, standing on the steps to Matie's house with Matie by her side watching the van being parked.

My house is getting crowded. Matie thought to herself as she scrutinized Amel'iya sliding out of the white Chevy van and sauntering up the front walk.

Sauntered like a panther, in no hurry but capable of springing into action in a split second Matie thought. Then she shook the silly notion out of her head.

Amel'iya came up to Susan and Matie (Matie was standing two steps up) and looked straight into Matie's eyes while extending her outstretched hand.

"I'm here. So fill me in," she said turning towards Susan.

"Enter and all will be revealed," Susan said which made Matie laugh. Something she hadn't done in a long time.

"After Susan gave her a comprehensive yet fast rundown (she's good at that, she's studying law and Amel'iya and her have this kind of shorthand mind thing going, as I've mentioned).

Susan then grabbed Casey, their bikes and gear from the van and went off for a ride up and down the hills around Gening.

Amel'iya was off to see the preacher man. Matie had gone to Springrock.

Me? I was busy putting together the information Casey needed that I had found down in the city. (Casey was being more specific in her requests or demands, whichever way you want to look at it. But it meant she was getting close.)

Two hours later, Susan and Casey were back, neither breathing hard or exhausted (we are trained good) when Amel'iya came back.

I stopped what I was doing and we all looked at her.

"He's scum," was all Amel'iya said as she passed us going to the kitchen to see what she could scrounge.

Susan nodded her agreement and followed Amel'iya into the kitchen for food.

Casey came over to my work area, which was crammed into a corner of the living room, and I started to show her what I had.

"Susan, you and I are going out early in the morning," Amel'iya said as she came back into the room with a large plate of salad stuff. Susan was already stuffing something into her mouth and did a double take at Amel'iya.

Susan swallowed and said, "Why?" after which she commandeered the right side of Matie's comfortable couch.

Susan doesn't waste too many words especially when one word does the trick.

"We're going to tail that little creep, and when he's occupied, you're going to be the look-out and I'm going to do a once over at the place where he lives."

Susan said nothing. Casey and I both said, "WHAT!"

Mia repeated, "WHAT!" totally startled at the turn of events. "Amel'iya was going to break into his apartment or house or whatever and search the place? But ... but that's illegal!"

"You're absolutely correct. It was all kinds of illegal.

Using her calm no nonsense manner voice, Susan also told Amel'iya it was illegal.

"And?" Amel'iya responded as though illegality was of no consequence.

Amel'iya looked at Susan, telling her in their secret language that she was going to search the place anyway, but she needed Susan.

"And Susan went? Didn't she?" Mia said, "Amel'iya used the magic word. She told Susan that she was needed. And when one of you says they need you, even if it's in a weird language thing, you all ask where, when and add, I'm on my way."

"That's Class '94 for you. "I said with a smile and nod of my head.

"I sometimes envy what you all have together."

"Up until someone turns out to be a dirty rotten traitor."

"O.K. I didn't mean to go there. So ... let's skip the traitor stuff and get back to what Amel'iya found. I know she found something. Didn't she?"

"His security wasn't high grade, but three locks are still a challenge. And then she found some intruder-tells that she had to go around and one she had to reset on the way out. She took a picture of everything she found and it showed a sophisticated set-up that I sent off to Washington to go over."

"And?"

"And the guy was dirty. We just had to find out how he was doing it and who was his target."

"But wasn't my great aunt his target?"

"That's where it got squirrelly. From what she was finding, your mom didn't think your great aunt was the primary target. And neither did my source. And even I was going in that direction. But almost everything was still pointing at the Reverend.

As for Amel'iya, she flat out said Matie wasn't his main target. And Susan agreed."

"Then Amel'iya said he's big game hunting. Susan nodded her head in agreement. Your mom, Matie and I probably looked like dear caught in the headlights of an oncoming car. A big game hunter in Gening?"

"What is she?"

"Amel'iya?" I asked.

"Yes! Amel'iya! Breaking into someone's apartment! That's like cop stuff or spy stuff. What is she?"

"She was a student and a racer as far as we knew then, but I guess she was into her trade craft even then. Some sort of operative or thief. Maybe. Like picking locks and spying on people. Maybe.

"That's a lot of maybe's"

"Well ... she did know a lot of Washington types, which is how she got to know what the agencies needed in the tech world. When I could figure out how to supply the upgrade or create the solution, she would patent and sell it. That money, and of course our scholarships, got us through all the education we stuffed into our heads. And helped Grace and the others too."

"And what is Amel'iya's trade craft?"

"Damn if I know."

56

Your great aunt was miserable. Your mom was knee deep in numbers and accounts, I was following the Ident trail, and Amel'iya and Susan were going over every bit of information we had so far, with a fine tooth comb, spending a lot of time huddled together out back going over their list of suspects for the rumors. (They also were out a lot, culling the population for every bit of gossip on their suspects.)

We'd gathered twice each day for a confab in order to make sure we hadn't missed any death threats while putting the pieces that we kept finding in their proper place.

So there we were at our evening confab listening to Susan and Amel'iya.

Susan and Amel'iya can get people to tell them the craziest stuff. That's how Jordon Betts got on their list of suspects.

They found out that Betts had a modest baritone voice, and he'd lead the congregation choir; that was until Matie was hired by the Church board. He was replaced.

They also found out that his friend JL did maintenance for the Church before your great aunt showed up. He was replaced too."

"And why didn't you keep them on?" Susan asked Matie as we all swiveled around to look at her.

"Oh my! I'd forgotten about them.

"Well, Jordon has a heavy hand with the way he charges for services and supplies while his friend JL is not particularly nice to women.

"Jordon does excellent work, but ... ."

"O.K. Jordon is not honest and his buddy JL is a misogynist. They're on our list by the way." Amel'iya looked at Susan who was taking notes. Susan just nodded back.

At the other end of town, it was after hours at Jordon's car repair business, (located in a small garage he rented for the purpose) when JL knocked at the back door.

Jordon, quickly stuck his head out of the open doorway after JL came through and looked out into the alley to see if anyone had followed his friend. After locking the door he put his hand on JL's back pushing him into the interior while asking, "What's going on?"

"We can get rid of her now, it's the perfect time. Everything's working in our favor," JL said.

"Are you sure this time?" Jordon asked.

"Last time was just a dry run."

"But we had to put the money back."

"This time she won't just be embarrassed and have people doubt her. Now we know how to do it." JL said, adding, "No woman belongs up there preaching at me. That ain't natural. She ain't natural. Woman who should be married and having babies," JL said as his friend nodded his head in agreement. "She won't get out of this one, I've made sure of that.

"How?" Jordon asked with mild skepticism.

"I've made sure," was all JL would say.

After a moment Jordon shrugged and asked, "O.K., how much do you think is in it?"

"I'm told there's probably over two thousand," JL answered.

"That's a lot of money JL."

"And we're go'n to split it."

"Yeah."

"O.K. You're sure? Right?"

"I'm sure."

"O.K., when are we going to do it? Jordon asked thinking about what he could do with a thousand dollars.

"After bible study on Sunday," JL said.

"O.K., you want some coffee? There's some on the burner. Then tell me again what I need to do," Jordon said as he poured them each a mug.

56

Some people think that chance is a funny thing. But chance is a trickster.

If you're a thief, you're usually surrounded by thieves, in a loose sort of way; so it's not unusual for one thief to cross the path of another thief. In fact it's almost inevitable.

And so, when he started his life of crime, the young huckster came across a more seasoned, more experienced, more polished con-man. A man who took the soon to be "fake preacher Charmeur" under his wings; teaching him the finer points of the swindle.

The first rule of the game was drilled into the young man until the words invaded his dreams.

Stick to your own people.

Don't go white; they have their own kind to cheat them; and they don't like any black man on their turf.

That's exactly what Josiah Fortis did. He was neither embarrassed, hesitant or ashamed. Black was his comfort zone, he knew it well; maneuvering between history and the present (which he saw as the same old oppression, racism and hatred repeated) with the ease that only comes from inbred familiarity surrounded by outside "no trespassing" barriers.

Young Josiah easily morphed into a preacher, with a new name, a brand new bought Christian preacher certificate, and a game plan.

By the time he was thirty, Preacher Charmeur had worked his way up to very profitable scams.

Comprised of an opening, a scapegoat, a target and an exit.

The scapegoat for his first gig was a black female university professor. The scapegoat for his second gig was a black female librarian.

For this gig, it would be Matie Cooper.

The prize would be the biggest one yet. He figured ten million minimum. (At the turn of the twenty first century, this was indeed a lot of money.)

Achieving this goal, was a far cry from the skinny hungry little boy, he once was. A traumatized boy who swore to himself, after that last beating he took at the hands of the man, who said he was his father, that he would find a way out. No man would ever beat up on him again. Beat him till he bled.

When the abused boy reached the age of eleven, he started with cheating and stealing; living rough and carefully working his way up. Never making the same mistake twice and keeping himself to himself.

At the age of fifteen he found his mentor; the man who taught him about swindles, con games and scams.

At the side of Gillis Marshall, he not only earned more money than he ever had at any given time, but he learned the ways of a world he didn't even know existed.

It was a realm where men stole from each other and didn't get caught.

Where men used inside information for their own benefit.

Where men could even murder and get away with it.

And then, he found out he was smart.

So smart, that people started paying him, a lot of money, to use those smarts.

This is when he found the ticket for entrance into the big game.

He said goodbye to Gillis, amicably, and headed out on his own.

He found computers and the wide open world it was attached to.

His greatest gift though, even more then he was smart, if you could call it a gift, was picking out his "sheepeople" from the herd. The supernumeraries floating around the periphery of his con games.

The type of humans (who exist in multitudes) who blame everyone else for what they didn't get, what they don't have, what they couldn't do, and for the unhappiness deep inside their very bones.

A man who could manipulate the minds of damaged dysfunctional people had "power". If they were damaged more by his actions, it wasn't his fault.

He never looked at what he did as hurting people; which made irresponsibility easy for him; which made it easy for him to discard humans with abandon, like tossing out food that's past it due date.

57

Preacher Charmeur walked with purpose, smiled a lot and paid attention to details as he went about setting himself up in Gening, New York; in the same manner as he had done twice before.

Following his proven gameplan, he'd come to town having already picked his mark and his fall-guy.

This time the fall-guy, he laughed at this, and said to himself, the fall-gal will be the Reverend Dr. Matie Cooper of the Springrock Baptist Church.

He had spent over four months planning and running the matches and the possibilities; going over every aspect in exquisite detail. The preacher man always planned ahead, always walked away clean from his projects.

That was his modus operandi. The one mantra he kept repeating to himself… the preacher man always walks away clean.

From his time culling the Reverend Dr. Cooper's parishioners, he'd found the emotionally needy, greedy, soaked in hatred, fear and in-securities types.

The people who couldn't stand to see anyone become successful; when they couldn't. The people who were so wretched with their own lives that they couldn't stand anyone else being happy. The type of people who dug around in the dirt of other people's lives gleefully turning the information into malicious gossip.

These maliciously thread-upon souls were his inner core.

Nikki Brown and Jaamika Jones were his first; then came Pace Betts and her brother Jordan Betts, Makay'la Krimbell, Jessea Baret and Stellie Nelson.

He augmented them with May Adams and her sister Spring from the Catholic Church. He found DeShawn Farley in the Episcopal Church. (DeShawn used to be at Springrock with his brother and sister-in-law, but left after the Reverend Dr. Cooper arrived.)

To fill out his estimated quota of fifty he not only insinuated himself into Gening's religious denominations but went into the Jehovah Witness and Evangelicals (who were the best blinded followers he had ever found).

He was like an art dealer rummaging through someone's attic separating the fakes from the real thing.

It rather amused him, that wherever he went there were plenty of assets to choose from. People who were trained from birth to lean on religion and to do as they were told by a parent, a priest, a boss or a partner.

They were followers; trained and prepped from birth.

People who hid behind their curtained windows, afraid of everything outside of the fence they surround themselves with.

People who refused to believe the truth. Who turned their backs to reality. Who didn't have any understanding or experience with responsibility. Who blamed others for consequences.

The last person he recruited was Michelle Goodwell, a woman who seemed most eager to join his inner group.

At first he was doubtful. She was somehow out of character, what with being irritatingly assertive. Also she asked a lot of questions.

Too many questions for comfort he first thought; but she didn't get upset when he side-stepped her inquires.

When he smiled while belittling her.

When he smiled while she let him put a collar around her neck.

Now JL, he didn't ask questions.

He was a silent angry large hulking soft bellied man now employed by a chain store that sold tires and did oil changes.

His chain store job was an ego deflating come-down compared to the top supervisory position he held for years at IBM. He lost this job after the company switched to "team employment". They created a new work force (except for their top brass) that were hired for two or three year contracts.

When his contract was over, he wasn't offered another one.

When not doing the mindless work scheduling appointments at the tire replacement store, he did minor car and small machine repairs in one of the units in the garage behind the three story run-down apartment building where he lived.

JL liked the new preacher man. The man showed him some respect.

Preacher Charmeur smiled: they like what I have to offer, they eat it up like candied liquor; gives them a shot at feeling important, being seen and given a recognizable (legitimate they believe) religious purpose to pump up their sense of self-importance and self-worth.

They'll never see it's all a lie. No one has before.

His brand new congregation sat before him, enraptured by his showmanship and ready to be fleeced.

And fleeced they were.

The first service of the Mercy Mission Congregation was a roaring success. He preached the god anointed wonders of mercy.

The salvation in the hereafter for giving, and the joy of the everlasting love that god bestows on believers. And of course he served up a side order of the wrath of god on the sinners; the non-believers.

For five months, he cloaked his hellfire and brimstones sermons in ambiguity laced with approved bigotry and justifiable racism (not just against white people but also people of their own race).

And then he gave them confirmation, that their choice, that their service to his Church, and the belief in his message were graced by god himself.

58

"**B**rothers and Sisters," He bellowed - drawing out each syllable in his baritone preacher voice, while flinging his arms outstretched wide to the heavens above, "We have raised over FIF ... TEEN ... THOU' ... SAND ... DOLLARS for the Pilma Village Mercy Fund."

A chorus of Halleluiahs reverberated in the small room.

"They will have their new well and clean drinking water, god willing in a few short months.

Hal-le-lui-ah!"

To which the congregation immediately raised their voices in response with a rousing, "Halleluiah and A' men."

"You have accomplished god's good work!"

"Halleluiah and Amen" reverberated in triumph.

"And for this coming month," he lowered his voice and leaned forward towards the congregation, for effect, "our Congregation will work towards building a brick factory, YES a strong brick factory ... for the good people of Marleewalah Village.

"Poor people who are star'vin ... yes I say star'vin. People who have no employment ... no way to feed their families." He declared in his deep missionary fervor voice.

The congregation sat in rapture. And the basket kept going around and around, as each week passed and as each month passed and as each good act of mercy followed the next.

The people of Pilma Village did get a well. A re-dug surface well that might last till the next drought. The people of Marleewalah Village did get a brick factory. A small wooden frame hut with one large mixing vat for mud and straw bricks.

For every dollar that went into his projects the good Preacher kept ninety-five cents.

Each month a flyer was handed out to his parishioners showing a generic picture of African people, Asian people, Pacific Island people or Indigenous people on one side. On the other side was a glossy picture in Technicolor of "a similar" project like the one they believed they were contributing to.

And in a special leather-bound book, he kept at the ready, were thank you letters from faraway places each mounted on heavy and expensive parchment. He always made sure to show anyone who was looking at the book all the empty pages in the back that were waiting to be filled with acts of mercy.

This would be his third Mercy Mission Congregation endeavor.

Knowing how a bad rep could follow you, he always left his parishioners in the hands of some good Church, in the vicinity, while he tearfully told his flock that he was off to do hands on missionary work in the jungles of South America, Africa or outer Mongolia. It didn't matter where, what mattered to his parishioners was that he loved them, and only the good works of helping others less fortunate could drag him away from them.

He made sure to say that he was going where no mail or phone could reach him; but upon his return, god willing - if he survived (he was sure to add) he would return to his congregation whom he loved with all his heart.

From the back of the little Mercy Mission Congregation Church Michelle smiled and said to herself, he'll do nicely.

Jordon and JL were also making plans as was Makay'la. The new preacher man seemed to fit all their needs.

59

We were all sitting around Matie's kitchen table when I opened my mouth. "Being around you Reverend and the church and all, I've been thinking on the color-of-Catholicism."

Matie looked at me with gross skepticism.

To be clear about who I was talking about, I went through a whole list from Calvinists, Shakers, Mormons, Baptist, Jehovah witness, Protestant, Greek or Russian orthodox - all of whom practice some form of Catholicism.

"Yes," Matie responded waiting for the punch line while Susan decided to ignore me and Casey gave me the evil eye thinking I was on the attack.

"Well … it's bewildering ! It staggers the imagination. Because all the white supremacists in these Christian sects are hanging their jock straps on the genitals of a dark skinned man."

Susan WAS paying attention! I heard her groan while trying not to laugh. Casey's mouth hung open, but no words came out. Amel'iya gave me one of her 'go girl' smiles. The Reverend? She laughed so hard we thought she was going to fall off her chair.

When everyone was back in the game I continued. "You know he couldn't have been a white man? I'm guessing here, but he most probably was a dark skinned Middle Eastern man, similar to his dark skinned Arab, Persian, Cannanite and Philistine neighbors?"

And then I added the punch line the Reverend Dr. Matie Cooper was waiting for, "For sure he was no fair-haired baby blue eyed Anglo-Saxon European dude."

Well that did it. The Reverend was gone, Susan was doubled over and Casey? Well Casey didn't know whether to laugh or kick me. I never did get a response from the Reverend because just then her doorbell rang.

The room fell silent.

Matie got up out of her chair and hesitantly went to the front door with Amel'iya right behind her.

Jaamika Jones was standing in the open doorway, with a group of two women and two men behind her.

"Hello Jaamika," Matie said hesitantly.

Without any formality, Jaamika proceeded to read her proclamation, "Reverend, where is the two thousand and eight dollars we've collected for the school project?"

Before Matie could answer, Casey came up and squeezed herself in front of her aunt and said, "Ms. Jones is it?"

"Yes it is, and I am talking to your aunt there behind you."

"Ms. Jones, if you want to come in, pleasant like, and have a seat, while your friends wait outside, I am sure we can figure out what you are talking about."

"What I'm talk'in bout ain't none of your business."

"Well actually it is Ms. Jones."

Jaamika was taken aback, but just for a moment.

"Explain yourself young woman. And where's your aunt?" She'd just noticed that Matie was now nowhere in sight. (Amel'iya had hauled Matie back into the living room.)

Then, Susan, stepped in front of Casey and said, "Ms. Casey is authorized and I am her lawyer. So, would you like to come in and talk about whatever is bothering you?"

Jaamika turned and looked at the people who had come with her. None of them seemed to want to go any further. She pulled up her pride to its fullest height and Susan and Casey stepped aside to let the woman storm in.

Casey looked at Susan with worry. Susan winked. Casey relaxed. A wink from Susan would hold the titanic up.

Amel'iya was now in the living room holding up a wall. Her arms crossed over her chest, looking down at the outraged woman who was probably a yard and a half shorter than Amel'iya.

When the brief conversation was over, Jaamika Jones left, with Matie, Susan, Casey, Amel'iya and me in tow. We all marched to the church; with Jaamika's followers close behind.

And sure enough the box was empty.

"I've called the police." Jaamika Jones announced.

60

The police chief himself was waiting at the rectory entrance. Not a good start we first thought. But it turned out all right in a crazy sort of way.

He went in with the good Reverend Dr. and they both wore those glove and shoe things that police wear to keep prints and whatever from being spoiled.

As it turned out, whoever had stolen the money, was not your expert invisible expert burglars.

"Burglars? You're telling me there were more than one?" Mia asked as I got up to go make a cup of tea.

"Yes my little goddaughter, burglars. Plural. 'Burglar Challenged burglars'."

"Oh come on Claire!" Mia said following me into my compact kitchen with its bright yellow walls and orange-indigo cabinets. She looked into the fridge for something but found nothing to her liking. I opened a cabinet door and handed her a tin of cookies.

Her eyes lit up.

As the water was boiling I turned to her and said, "'Burglar Challenged burglars' came straight out of the well of wisdom owned and operated by our Amel'iya."

"Burglar challenged? That's kind of ridiculous." Mia said, in a cookie-crunching-in-her-mouth sort of way.

"I will describe the scene and you can decide if a person or persons, are burglar challenged.

"First, a bottle was knocked off the Reverend's table and replaced, in the wrong position (with burglar fingerprints).

"Second, a few faint but visible boot prints were found (with car oil and grease imbedded in the rug).

"And then, a ten-dollar bill (with a burglar fingerprint on both sides of one corner where the bill was held as it was wiped clean.) It was found in Matie's top desk drawer by the chief himself (money from the stolen money everyone presumed; probably trying to show that Matie stole the money but maybe dropped a bit into her desk drawer).

"Oh, and the doorknob was wiped clean but there was a print on the door frame. And the desk drawers were wiped clean, but there was a half print left on the money box."

"Oh come on! No ones that's ..... can I use the word stupid?"

"Ridiculous, absurd, even asinine would work here."

"O.K. . Let's stick with Burglar challenged." Mia said, and we smiled at each other.

I walked back to my command center with Mia, cookie in hand, behind me. She dropped into her seat and said, "How did Jaamika even know the money was missing? And wasn't the place locked? I mean how did she get into the place to even know that the money was gone?"

"Ah! All good questions. First, Matie swore that she'd locked up the whole church good and tight after bible study. Yet, when we came to the rectory door, it was unlocked.

"When Jaamika was asked how she knew the money was gone she hesitated for a moment."

"Ms. Jones?" the police chief said (asking the belligerent woman that exact question).

"Well I got a call. Someone out of breath. And he just said the Reverend took the money. Saw her do it."

"And who was the caller?"

"Well ... how should I know? He just said his piece and hung up; and then I called my friends, and we all went over here."

"And how did you get in?"

"Well, the door was open of course. What'd you think? That I broke in or something!" she said trying to sound outraged, and not succeeding.

"Chief," the fingerprint guy said.

"What?"

"The door handle has been wiped clean, but there's a pretty clear set on the edge of the doorframe where someone grabbed it."

"And?"

"And, I'd say it looks like it matches some of the prints I've already found in strange and mysterious places. And there's a lot of trying to wipe prints off.

"And, they don't match the Reverend's. She was real nice about letting me have a set."

"How about we go find out whose prints they are," the chief said.

"By this time Jaamika Jones, and her bilious pride, were collapsed onto a step outside the building. We think she took a hit with the cake sale money fiasco and wanted to get back her own. Or else she was just .... None of us wanted to put any foul language into the air around the good Reverend Dr. Matie Cooper, so we refrained from any name calling.

(We were to learn later that the good Reverend Dr. Matie Cooper knew more foul language (that she used most liberally) than all of us combined. We were impressed.)

"O.K. let me guess," Mia said as the wheels started to turn. "The tire man who had a garage where he did repairs? And his buddy. Am I right?"

"You pegged them all right. J.L. and his buddy Jordon."

"But how did they get in?"

"One of them didn't turn in their key when they were fired. They said they lost it. And Matie never got around to changing the locks. It's kind of like something you really should do; like immediately after moving into a place. "

"That's kind of .. ?"

"Not too bright?"

"Well we all make mistakes."

"Yes we do."

"But WHY? Why did they do it?"

"I'm getting to that. Patience my little godchild." Mia gave me one of her mother's looks. She was getting pretty good at it.

But first I needed get back to David.

61

"Oh Shit!" I jumped up so fast the chair I was sitting on went flying.

"WHAT!? Amel'iya yelled.

"That was David."

"And?" Susan demanded.

"He got hold of the autopsy and you are not going to believe this."

"Give us a try." Amel'iya was in her snide mode at the moment.

"The kid, Malcolm Farley, was chloroformed and then shot up with some really old shit. Like some twenty year old junk."

"We knew he was murdered. So wh…. ? OH!" The penny dropped.

"So Susan… he was murdered to set up the Reverend or make her appear complicit somehow. The kid had a drug problem. Matie got involved. So someone was trying to make the connection look like she was responsible for his death; by drugs."

"Not only is someone out to ruin the Reverend" Amel'iya summarized, "but they might be out to do her some really long lasting harm. Or kill her."

"You're crazy! Kill her!" I blurted out.

We all sat there stone silent for a moment.

Then Susan asked, "Are we going to tell her and Casey?"

After another really awkward moment of silence and looking at each other I threw up my hands. I was overwhelmed, "Oh Shit. I don't know." I whispered.

"The Reverend is not going to believe she's actually in harm's way and Casey … well Casey'll go crazy scared for her aunt." Amel'iya summarized again. "But the Police Chief knows this too, he does get forensic reports you know ... so ... I'm thinking that's the real reason we have a cop outside all the time and another one who escorts her to and from the church."

"This is getting ... I don't know what this is getting, but I don't like it one bit. And I'm telling Casey." Susan announced.

"What Susan decides, Susan does. She waited until the Reverend had to go to the Church for one of her group talks and we cornered Casey.

"Your mom went ballistic.

"Amel'iya waited until Susan had your mom seated and with a stiff drink firmly held in her shaking hands before she added, "We need to sit your aunt down when she gets back and get some more history on the people she's told us about and see if there are anymore dungbunnies hanging around. Personally, I think Charmeur is part of this whole thing. His set up at his apartment is not the usual set up for a plain religious man, or any law abiding man for that matter."

"This crushed your mom and me. Susan? Not so much.

"Amel'iya got up and walked out."

"Dungbunnies?" Mai was shaking her head back and forth, rolling her eyes and generally making like this was totally ridiculous.

"You need to remember, we were still in the state of "bad language denial"."

"But Dungbuinnies?"

"Amel'iya can ... could be very inventive when she chose to be." I said with some bad feelings and ignited hatred coming to the surface.

"O.K. let's forget about the language thing. O.K.?

I gave her a half smile. That was about all I could do. It still hurt to remember how Amel'iya had betrayed us.

62

Matie, having seen her group off, walked up to Amel'iya, who was now sitting in the back row of the empty church. She sat down next to her.

"I think religion is like a very large picture book for young children," Amel'iya said

"Interesting imagery. If It's just a picture book to amuse kids, what do you, as an adult, think religion is about?"

Amel'iya kept looking down the rows of empty seats and smiled, "Religion is about men who don't want to get their hands dirty or their backs broken by doing hard, but honest labor for their daily bread."

She paused for a moment and then continued, "I think it's about men and control.

"A long time ago some guy said religion was for the masses. I think he said it was the opioid of the masses. Like that's how you control them. I don't normally agree with the junk that comes out of men's brains – but this guy was right on target."

Amel'iya looked sideways at the reverend, "But you're not into control are you? You're into spirituality; the unknown, the connection we have with the unknown and the universe as a whole."

Susan and I, had just snuck into the church, wiggling ourselves into a pew a few rows behind the Reverend and Amel'iya; far enough away not to alert them but close enough to hear the rest of what they were talking about. (Of course Amel'iya knew we were there. She has eyes in the back of her head and ears that can pick up a signal from the other side of the galaxy.)

I was spellbound. Susan not so much.

"I'm just glad we don't live in the time of Peter." Amel'iya said off-handedly.

"Matie looked over at Amel'iya. I held my breath."

"Peter 1:7, Corinthian 3:13, trial by fire: Every man's work shall be made manifest: for the day shall declare it, because it shall be revealed by fire; and the fire shall try every man's work of what sort it is."

The Reverend looked sideways at Amel'iya and said, "That was perfect! Word for word.

"The way I understand it," Amel'iya continued, "these trials will show that your faith is genuine. Your faith is being tested as fire tests and purifies gold--though your faith is far more precious than mere gold. So when your faith remains strong through many trials, it will bring you much praise and glory and honor on the day when Jesus Christ is revealed to the whole world. I think that's the way it goes."

"Just to make a comment here," The Reverend said, "I'm glad that we don't literally do trials by fire anymore.

"It was most assuredly barbaric." Amel'iya said. "A test in which a person is set on fire in order to assess his/her truthfulness, commitment, courage, etcetera, is beyond inhuman, it's ..."

"It's hard to fathom in modern context." the Reverend said.

"Not really Reverend. It's the men of the church doing their thing." Amel'iya said with no accusation in her voice just in a matter of fact way.

"One day Reverend, white men will take away all our rights ... and women will lose all the gains they have achieved; like voting. Even the right to have an abortion will be outlawed again.

"One day Reverend we will be living under a theocratic regime where both black men and white men subjugate women.

"Have you read the "Handmaid's Tale by Margaret Atwood?" Amel'iya asked Matie.

"No. But I will be sure to ready it now."

Amel'iya tilted her head, looked at the Reverend who was smiling at her and smiled back shaking her head in acceptance.

Amel'iya was not finished.

"Look at the Baptist commitment to male patriarchy. They say black men are the law in their own homes and that their women are to be subservient and supportive to men.

"In their minds, men are the ones to preach down on woman. And the men of the Baptist hierarchy will one day proclaim, like their great-grandfathers proclaimed, that women don't belong in the pulpit; because women should never be the ones preaching down on men.

"When this happens, mark my words, all Baptist pulpits will be reserved only for men. Woman will be shut out, for good this time."

"Are you sure?" Matie asked as though Amel'iya might be right.

"Yeah. I'm sure. Reverend, in the real world, men rule - unless there's a problem, then most times they hire a woman outright to fix it, at woman-pay. Then when it's fixed they fire her or if things fail, she's the scapegoat. Most times they hire a man who has a smart woman working for him, at woman-pay, who does the heavy lifting and saves the day, but she is still fired. Or, shifted over to an out of the way position where she earns no credit and still gets woman-pay.

"Reverend, I think you found an anomaly here and took advantage of it. You slipped in and I bet the same thing happened to the few other women in your profession. You all found some anomaly. And I bet each and every one of you works ten times harder and longer hours, doing more of the heavy lifting than any man behind a Baptist pulpit."

The Reverend didn't answer Amel'iya right away. After a long silent moment Amel'iya turned all the way around, stared at us and said, "I'm right, aren't I?"

"Maybe." I whispered. I never cross Amel'iya when she is into the inequalities perpetrated on women by men.

"Right as ever." Susan said.

Casey who had come in by this time sat behind Susan and me. She said nothing. She knew what was coming.

The Reverend turned around Mia, and smiled at your mom, Susan and me.

"I am going to leave the future up to all of you." She said, and then added something that made me smile, "The one thing I do know is that one day, no one is going to "woman-pay" you Amel'iya … and … if you have anything to do with it neither will any of Class'94."

"Right on Reverend." Amel'iya said. "Now Reverend I have to tell you what we've found out so far.

"I'm not going to like this part? Am I?" Mia asked, scrunching up her face like she had just smelled something vile.

"Actually your great aunt said nothing."

"Nothing?"

"After Amel'iya finished talking, your great aunt stood up, very slowly, and walked out into the aisle. She turned back to us, looked at each of us and then said, "So … my reputation and my job are at stake. And what is going on may qualify as vicious the way you put it … which might, you think, escalate into physical harm; which I can't see happening by the way. But. O.K.. Now that I know evil's knocking at my front door, it's time to fight back."

And then she turned and walked out of the church. Back straight and with purpose.

I sat there like a dummy. My head was starting to hurt. Your mom ran after your great aunt.

"Get up Claire Elizabeth, we have work to do." These were Amel'iya's exact words.

I made my feet work and got up. That's what Class'94 does when one of us gives an order.

Susan was already standing.

We locked up the church and walked back to Matie's house as Susan and Amel'iya started to discuss what we were going to do next. I trailed behind them, silently. I was still working on what your mom and I had found out.

63

FIRE! Amel'iya sat bolt upright staring into the darkness. Then the back of the house exploded.

"FIRE!" she screamed again and reached for Susan while kicking me.

Then the commands came. "Susan – outside, get the hose out front, turn it on and hose the inside stairs down. Claire call fire and police. NOW!"

Without a moment's hesitation, Amel'iya charged up the staircase screaming for Casey and Matie to wake up. By the time I fumbled and found my cell, and looked up, I saw that Amel'iya had bolted up the stairs.

I was screaming into the phone when I saw the three of them at the top of the stairs with fire behind them; I almost passed out.

Then Matie turned around and headed back into her bedroom with Casey behind her.

"FUCK!" was all Amel'iya said as she too disappeared.

I was still yelling into the phone but trying to give the correct information to the 911 operator while my heart was pouring terror into my brain.

The next thing I saw was Matie slung over your mom's shoulder, like a rag doll and Amel'iya holding a bible in one hand and gripping Casey's Tshirt with the other; guiding her down the stairs.

The smoke was so bad that your mom was coughing and I don't think she could see that well. I heard Amel'iya giving her step by step orders.

I held out one hand towards Casey while Susan continued to hose me, the stairs and the foyer. I was at the dripping buckets stage.

As soon as your mom, with her aunt still slung over her shoulder, was close enough I reached out and took a firm grip on her arm and pulled her outside.

"A Bible!" Mia exclaimed

"Yeah, a freakin bible. Your great aunt went back for the Cooper bible. Amel'iya said she'd toss any bible for any of Shere Hite's books.

"But that particular bible was the most precious item your aunt had from her marriage. It was a tangible link to her dead husband, a man she loved. So, she was not going to leave it behind."

"But … but …"

"Right, the place was on fire. But she was not leaving without it and Casey was not leaving without her aunt and Amel'iya was furious at both of them."

"Why was my mom carrying Matie?"

"Remember. There was a fire?"

"OH! Yeah!"

"So stuff falls in fires. And something fell and knocked Matie out. Casey said it was something big. That was all she remembered. Her aunt was on the floor so she made a fast grab for the bible, tossed it to Amel'iya, and then hauled Matie over her shoulder and down the stairs they came."

"As soon as they were out of the burning building, Amel'iya grabbed the hose and rinsed her eyes out and pulled Casey's head back and flushed her eyes while Susan ran out to the street to direct the ambulance people towards Matie. She was lying on the ground with her head in Casey's lap.

Her eyes were closed and Casey was frantic."

"Oh Shit! Someone tried to kill them!" Mia was up and pacing not knowing what to do with the sudden attack off fear.

I got up and grabbed her and held on.

"Mia it's OK. Really. We were all fine. Matie was out for a few hours, and had to stay in hospital for two days, but we all got out! O.K.?"

Then she started crying. And I stood there like a dummy holding the kid and rubbing her back. I'd seen it done by her mother, so I figured it might work here.

64

"What happened next?" Mia asked, after taking a break to splash some cold water on her face.

"Next?" I asked her; since she sounded like "next" was something she really kind of didn't want to know.

"Yeah." She said taking a deep breath and letting it out - slowly. (She knew there was more or I have a "tell".)

I rolled my eyes while twisting my mouth to the left. I was displaying my reticence. Mia grabbed her chair handles. She was ready for the ride.

"Mr. Powell, the old one, came storming into the hospital having pushed the detective on duty aside. Well not quite aside, the detective was hanging onto Mr. Powell's jacket. Powell came storming into the room with steam coming out of his ears and red hot darts shooting out his eyes.

He walked over to Matie and dropped a photograph in her lap. He starting calling her all the names in the book from whore to bitch. And ... he also swore she would never preach in "his" church again. And that he would find a man to do the job properly."

Mia moved up to the edge of her chair, eyes wide.

"I wasn't there mind you, but your mom and Amel'iya gave Susan and me a blow by blow account."

"What was his problem? Oh forget that, what did my great aunt do?"

" Your great aunt calmly picked up the picture, took a good look at it and looked up at Del Powell and laughed. She laughed so loud, she almost fell out of the hospital bed."

"LAUGHED!?" Mia shouted incredulously.

"She may still have had some pain killers running around in her head or she just lost it." I offered.

"And … ?", She stretched out the word as long as it would go. She sounded angry.

"And your great aunt ripped a new one for Old man Powell. The picture was of her and Powell's son in what looked like a sexual embrace.

"Nathanial Powell and his wife Jacqulyn, who was your great aunt's best friend, were both devastated at the time the picture was take.

Their young son was in a coma. He's been badly hurt in a car accident.

"So where do a lot of people go when something awful happens to them?"

"To church." Mia responded. I shook my head in agreement.

"Jacklyn Powell came to the church with her husband, Nathanial, to pray for their son and maybe find a little solace. Nathanial fell apart, Jacqulyn had collapsed into one of Matie's chairs and was crying her eyes out. Matie grabbed Nathanial who was about to fall down where he stood. He grabbed onto your great aunt and from what I was told fell to crying on her shoulder.

"And Nikki Brown took a picture."

"Nikki Brown?"

"Yeah, she was one of Matie's flock who flew away to the new preacher's nest."

"But how did Matie know it was her?"

"Matie caught a glimpse of her out the window when Nikki took the picture."

"So she always knew Nikki had taken a picture of them together?"

"That's what she told us later."

"Why didn't she say anything at the time?"

"She wouldn't tell us; but of course Amel'iya found out. She found out that Nikki was supposed to marry the man who some of the Board at Springrock wanted to give the pulpit to. But that was before your great aunt showed up.

"And your great aunt kind of felt sorry for her and didn't want to stir up the dust."

"It seemed the congregation loved your great-aunt right from the very first. And maybe, your great aunt might have thought to bring it up sometime in the future. Whatever."

Mia gave me one of her sweetest and biggest smiles. "She is a great reverend. Don't you think?"

"Absolutely. One hundred percent great." I smiled back.

"O.K., back to the hospital. What happened after my great aunt laughed at him?"

"Let's see if I can remember. (I had to think on this a minute.) O.K. she told him something like – 'Del, your grandson was in the hospital, this hospital actually, and he was in a coma. Your son and daughter-in-law were half crazed and came to the church to pray. Your son collapsed in my arms. One of our congregants was outside and took a picture through the window. I always wondered where it would end up and had almost forgotten about it until you came in with it.' "

"That's pretty good memorization. I'm impressed." Mia said.

"There was a lot more actually. Matie added some stuff in there about believing false rumors and other stuff she said to the old man but she's sure he didn't hear any of it. In fact she thought that all he actually heard was her laughing at him.

Amel'iya was leaning up against the wall, arms crossed over her chest, as usual, surveying the scene, and said, "You shouldn't have laughed at him Matie."

Matie didn't understand what Amel'iya was talking about. Matie was in the clouds, floating around somewhere as her eyes closed and she wandered off."

Mia looked expectantly at me.

"Laughing at a man most often makes them mean and all kinds of nasty all the way over the edge to vicious. It has something to do with their make-believe or made-up manhood image thing. Laughing at them acts like a long fat hot poker harpooning their egos. Not pretty."

"My dad once told me that men who are misogynists aren't good men and that I should stay away from them. He never told me about the laughing thing."

"I'd follow his advice. Your dad is one of the good ones. When your mom or one of us laugh at some ridiculous man-thing he does, he just laughs with us."

"He is, isn't he? One of the good guys I mean." She smiled.

I smiled back in acknowledgement.

65

Amel'iya was standing against the wall again. She does a lot of that.

Matie was feeling better and sitting up in her hospital bed, your mom was sitting next to your great aunt and Susan and I were in the background. Amel'iya was in her "listen up" mood with her arms crossed over her chest. She was looking at Matie when she said, "I think god's troubling the waters here in Gening New York."

Three pairs of eyes bulged open in astonishment. Matie sat frozen, her face a mask of confusion.

"The preacher man opened Pandora's box Reverend."

Susan, who can regain her equilibrium faster than a high powered bullet stood up and took a step forward to get your great aunt's attention, "It appears as though he released the seven deadly sins as a diversion."

"What are you two talking about?" Matie was not only confused but on the verge of anger. Bad combination.

Susan plowed on, "We have two concurrent events going on here. One is the character assignation and the other is a deep scam being played by the Preacher. A scam that looks like, according to our digital sleuth (she nodded towards me) and our numbers sleuth (she nodded towards Casey) involves old man Powell.

"Particulars coming to light as we speak."

Susan crossed the room to sit in the other visitor's chair.

She leaned towards Matie and continued, "Scheme A: Obfuscation using parishioners. People apparently steeped in the seven deadly sins

… maybe even eight sins according to my calculations. To be precise – gluttony, lust or fornication, greed or avarice or envy, sorrow or despair, vain glory, pride or hubris and sloth (I found this very interesting, it seems 'sloth' comes from monks who were and probably are indifferent to their duties).

Matie was lost in the woods somewhere. So was I. Casey not so much.

"Are lust and fornication really a sin?" I asked. Everyone looked at me as though I had just popped into the room, as if by magic.

"There's always a bit of lust going around in the congregation," Matie was back. "And yes, she added, "according to some of the written text fornication qualifies as a sin."

"You can tell us about that later." Susan interrupted, knowing I was about to go into this unbridled sex thing.

"I'm starting with greed. It's the easy one." Susan said.

"Charmeur, and this probably isn't his real name, is running a con on Del Powell."

Matie made a strangled gasp.

"To make this fast and succinct, old man Powell is a misogynist who is pilfering money from his company. The preacher found out by digging, like Claire has dug, and it looks like the preacher changed his plan from plain wiping out the man's bank accounts to blackmailing him. Big Time blackmail."

Matie's jaw dropped open but no words fell out. Just a squeak.

"I'll take wrath." Amel'iya said. "That one goes to Michelle. She was consumed with hatred over her husband's death. Blamed you Reverend.

"For a lot of women it's easier blaming another woman than the low-lead dung they're married to."

Matie went stone silent with that one.

"Nikki ?" Susan continued, "probably unbridled Pride. She lost face when that fiancé of her scampered off to better pastures.

"I think both Stellie and Nikki were also reeking of envy. I mean Stellie's brother was passed over for the position of Reverend. As for

Nikki, she didn't get to marry the head of Springrock Baptist Church. They probably talked themselves into blaming you for becoming Reverend at Springrock.

"It's a power thing. They have none, but if they became the sister or the wife of a Reverend, of one of the finest churches on the east coast, that would have given them the clout they could bargain with.

"The man represented status to two women. He disappointed them, but they chose to put the blame on you Matie for his not being good enough for the position and then leaving."

"Oh my Lawd!" Matie said placing a hand over her heart..

"I'll take the dynamic duncey-duo, Jordon and JL. They're plain and simple hateful, spiteful, misogynists. They don't think women have any place behind a pulpit. Or anywhere else as far as I can tell."

"Misogyny's not one of the deadly sins," Matie said softly.

"Should be the first!" Susan said. "How about hate, spiteful and a bit of sloth?"

"That would do it." Matie said, as she tried a half crooked smile towards Susan.

"Jealousy with Makayla." Amel'iya said.

"Pride with Jaamika," I offered

"Sloth again, but this time with DeShawn Farley. He is lazy while his second cousin Mr. Farley is gluttonous and needs to lose some of that huge roll he has around his middle." Susan chimed in. "Did Mr. Farley go over to the preacher's new church like his second cousin?"

"No." Matie said emphatically. "Mrs. Farley wouldn't hear of changing out of Springrock. It's not just religion or community with her. We're her family. Everyone has pulled together to help her since Malcolm was murdered.

"She can't understand why anyone would be so cruel, so evil, as to take her boy's life

"I can't understand it either."

Amel'iya tried to refocus the conversation. "We still have vain glory and sorrow or despair,"

"Let it rest girlfriend," I said.

Amel'iya looked at each of us and said as she started to walk out the door. "I'm going back to the house. Take a look around."

She made a nod at Susan who returned it. Matie was not going to be left alone. Amel'iya and Susan had made a scheldule so that two of us were always with Matie as long as she was in the hospital. Like guarding her.

Susan and Casey were up. I needed some sleep. I followed Amel'iya back. A sleeping bag in the back of the van had my name on it for the next six hours.

After we left, Casey said, "I think the seven deadly sins kind of covers what's going on here, except I never thought that lust was a sin. I just think it's gotten a rotten name because some people blame it or are afraid of it."

"Matie looked over at her niece in mock astonishment and Susan laughed. Susan told us later that your mom, realizing what she had just said, in front of her aunt, turned a shade of scarlet that's probably not in any tube of pain Whitney uses." I said smiling at Mia.

"Mom really said that? She thinks lust is O.K.?"

"Yes, but you didn't hear it from me."

"But she said you could tell me about what happened."

"You know she didn't mean for me to tell you that."

"But you did!" Mia said, as I could see the wheels turning so fast I could smell the burn.

"Pay attention! I'm mov'in on.

"JL also fit the bill for gluttony." I told Mia. "But Matie thought he made a better fit in the despair column."

"She didn't tell us why, but Amel'iya told us afterwards, when Matie wasn't around, that JL has a drug habit tripping him up all the time."

"Is being hooked on drugs gluttony?" Mia was puzzled.

"Anything you gorge on until you explode and die is gluttony in my dictionary."

"OK I'll buy that, how about laziness? Is that kind of sloth?" Mia asked.

"Susan of course would say it was and she'd also tell you that ignorance is just plain laziness. That's one of her red button issues."

"No one ever argues with Susan do they?" Mia asked.

"When Susan talks, the skies part. And she is almost always right. In fact, I don't think she's ever been wrong. I'll have to ask Grace the next time I see her. Grace knows stuff like that."

"I can see greed. The other ones are kind of wet wool. But there must have been a lot of greed at Springrock. A lot of them were rich? Right?" Mia asked with one of her cute smiles.

"That is exactly what Amel'iya said, which is probably why the preacher man chose the place. Plump pickings.

The interesting part I found out, what with my digital poking around, was that there were emails between Del Powell and Charmeur."

"WHAT!" The little tweenie stammered.

66

"The church money missing from the bank and then showing up was just the first punch. Nothing fancy just a snatch and dump but it did leave a signature. I'm real good with stuff like that Matie." I said looking at Matie who had no idea of what I was talking about.

"It's like a fingerprint, but digital. No two people write code in exactly the same way. Unless they are good forgers. And even then, I can usually ident them."

Matie had a very skeptical look on her face, like maybe I was an alien or something.

Let's skip along to the identity theft. Then the preacher started to pull his scam Long story short, David gave me the creds to get into the preacher's and Dale Powell's accounts, emails and files."

Now Matie shook her head at me.

"O.K. I did a little snooping on my own. But it worked!" I protested.

"You broke the law." Matie was mad. "What if you were caught. What would have happened to all of you? You could have been thrown out of college and lost your scholarships and all!"

"No one can catch Claire Elizabeth." Amel'iya flatly stated. Her face and body language giving nothing away. With this we all rolled our eyes at each other without moving or twitching; especially not reacting to what Amel'iya just said.

"Please continue." Susan said in a matter of fact voice.

"WAIT! WAIT A MINUTE! Mia squealed.

As soon as I said that about Amel'iya I knew, I just knew Mia was going to jump on it like an elephant on a mouse. An elephant who wasn't one bit scared of a little tiny mouse.

"Amel'iya is kind of weird. Leave it at that. And I am very good at what I do. Always have been."

"Well O.K. . I mean you have patents and all that, and your set-up here is like above and beyond high tech, and then there was that thing with the government …but not get caught!?"

"Mia, I get hired to do the catching and build the programs. I don't get caught."

"How does a woman get that much power in the shark infested male waters of the tech industry? Talk about jealousy. Jealousy aimed at women. Jealousy like what my aunt experienced in Gening."

"It's a matter of being better, even though Amel'iya always said being the best is essential." Mia was still skeptical. "I have a lawyer who is one step above lethal when it comes to contracts and making deals for me." I confessed.

"Better than Amel'iya was?"

"In a class by herself. She's like the Reigning Crone of Contracts. And she's so good that she can get me out of anything. Also, I know people like David that I do stuff for and I can call in a favor if I have to. So do you want the rest of the story?"

"Lawyer and favors. That I can buy."

"So do you want the rest of the story? I repeated.

"Can't wait." Mia said. I know she was trying not to laugh.

"I found the targeted account."

"Of course." Mia said off handedly. I squinted my eyes at her, she smiled at me, I continued. "And then I found the emails.

"It turned out that Charmeur had found out that Dell happened to be a tax manipulator, a pilferer. Plus the guy was a world class misogynist. (I didn't tell Mia or anyone else about the pornography.) As for Charmeur? He had a pigeon on a skewer ready to roast when I tagged him.

"Tax?"

"The tax thing was squirrelly. I didn't understand it. Dell was very rich, no doubt about that. But he was doing a lot of fancy tax-footwork according to your mom, as well as embezzling. Like he was stealing all over the place. Like he had an addiction or something.

"Why Dell was avoiding taxes big time, and doctoring the books, is still a mystery to me. He didn't have to do any of that to be rich.

Susan offered an explanation, if you're interested."

"All ears." the tweenie said.

"To someone as rich as Dell, scheming and scamming and always wanting more just comes with the territory. Men like him take as much as they can and then they go and take some more. It's an addiction that comes with wealth.

"So there is your great aunt, having survived an attempt on her life, finding out that the big honcho man in her church, was a thief and even worse."

"What could be worse than that?" Mia asked.

"We didn't tell your great-aunt about the connection between the preacher and Dell where Dell paid the preacher to get Matie Cooper out or Springrock. That was before the preacher started to clean out Dell's hidden accounts.

"I think it would've broken her heart. Of course she found out eventually, but we just couldn't tell her that her best friend's father-in-law was colluding with the make-believe preacher; not when we'd just escaped with our lives from a burning building and what with your your great aunt in a hospital bed."

"The preacher and this Powell person? They were connected?"

"The thread your mom found lead me to all sorts of stuff; especially the emails. I found out that Dell Powell was not only ready to pay off the preacher to keep silent about what he did, and remember that Dell didn't know the preacher was about to start cleaning out some of his hidden accounts, but he was willing to pay the preacher much more if the Rev. Dr. Maddie Cooper was thrown out of 'his' church."

"What? I thought I heard you wrong just a minute ago." Mia stammered.

"It turned out that Dell Powell was a raving misogynist and he believed that Springrock belonged to him. Every brick and stick of wood. And he wanted Matie out."

"Shit!

"Exactly."

"So how did my great aunt get the job in the first place? I mean Dell was the man?"

"She was invited to do a month of services. I think Dell and his minions really believed that she'd crash and burn and that would stop the talk about a woman in the pulpit from a lot of the congretation."

"She's good isn't she?" Mia smiled at me.

"Pretty damn good." I smiled back and nodded my head.

"I don't think I'm ever going to talk about this with my great-aunt."

"I think that is a very wise decision."

"So what happened?"

"Your aunt gave one of her riveting sermon the Sunday after the fire; after which the Chief came to tell Matie that the preacher had fled. He also told her that the Feds had a warrant out for him."

"Did he get any money? Ya' know the stuff in those hidden accounts."

"As a matter of fact he did. It was a really good heist if I must say so myself."

"Did he get away with it?"

I didn't answer.

"He didn't did he. You or this David person went after it and took it back. Right? Right? I'm right aren't I?" She insisted.

"All I'll say is that the money was retrieved, not that it did Dell any good."

"You stole it back! Wow!"

I didn't say anything. I was looking up at the ceiling.

"O.K. so what happened then?" Mia asked, bringing my attention back down to earth.

"Well ... before the police chief left he took your mom aside and told her he was really sorry, but the entire Mercy Mission Flock was convinced that the Reverend Matie Cooper was responsible for Malcolm's death, the stolen money, and, that all the rumors about her were true – no matter how much he and his detective told them otherwise.

"He also told her if there was any trouble to get in touch him, immediately.

"When she heard about this, Amel'iya did the interpretation: The trouble that the preacher let loose in Gening wasn't over by a long shot and the Reverend needed to take some serious precautions or find another flock to preach to.

"Your mom was ready to give up college right there and then, give up racing and basically her life and come live in Gening and watch out for her aunt."

"Oh Lordy Lordy." Mia exclaimed, "what a mess!"

67

"What happened next?" Mia asked with a weird squished face that I couldn't interpret. But it didn't look comfortable.

So, I just rolled ahead, "Next came the sermon that took the house and Dell Powell down.

"That was the next Sunday.

"Now you have to remember that the preacher had taken off, maybe not with all the money he wanted, but he had gotten his hands on the hidden stuff and Dell Powell must have known that by the time Sunday rolled around. And he must have been spitting angry and I bet really stressed out.

"As for us? When your great aunt gave that sermon she had moved in with good friends two blocks from her home. People who'd offered her their spare room.

"The four of us where bed rolling out in the van, like forever it seemed out there in front of the friend's house. I never want to do that again.

"By-the-way, Chief Wojick was certain that the preacher had set the fire but there was that nasty thing called evidence and proof, which he and his force were still chasing." I paused and took a deep breathe before I dove into the next part.

"I'd never seen that thing that religious people are supposed to have. That look like they've been touched with righteousness and the spirit. But your great aunt had it that morning."

"Mattie walked up to the pulpit in her perfect preacher attire. She walked straight as an arrow and as supremely confident as always in her own person and her faith.

"She stood there for a long moment looking out at the congregation, going from left to right. It was so quiet in the church that the only thing you could hear was the soft hum of the ventilation system.

"The congregation, that filled the Church up to the rafters, were glued in their spots.

"The Reverend Dr. Matie Cooper took her time looking at each person with love and compassion, nodding her head along the way.

"I'm telling you that we saw tears in many a stalwart faces.

"Your mom had told us that the Reverend had struggled with the short text she planned to deliver that day.

"She finally chose Peter 1:7 - the test of fire and Corinthian 3:13 - the trial by fire because her ministry, and the congregants, had come through a destructive crisis of faith with fortitude and love.

"Amel'iya smiled to herself. I saw it. Your great aunt had picked the words Amel'iya had quoted when they were talking in the church, and Amel'iya was gloating. I gave her a gentle elbow." She ignored it and me.

The whole congregation had almost the whole story by now. They knew about the preacher, the hateful gossip, evil rumors, the made up accusations about stealing and then Malcolm's death. They were all there to show their support. Well almost everyone.

In the total silence that pervaded the assembly the Reverend Cooper raised her voice and began:

"As we move into the uncertain future, from the tumultuous past, we struggle to keep our resolve firmly on the path of righteousness, kindness and compassion. We may lose our way as the trials become steeper. We may lose our way as the tribulations cut deeper. But we will persevere." When she paused she was looking directly at Dell Powell.

"Amen." came a resounding reply from the congregation not yet noticing what was really going on.

She looked back up and out to the congregation and her voice filled the church, "I have just passed through a trial of lies, a test by fire. And my faith and my commitment held true." Once again her eyes fell on Dell Powell.

"Amen." – came the chorus of voices.

"I was not alone in this test. Everyone here has been shaken down to their core This congregation and all the souls who sit here today have also been tested.

"Most of you have walked through the fire with courage and truthfulness and have come out stronger." She paused again looking down at Dell Powell.

"There are those among us who have come through this hard time holding our belief in ourselves and the righteousness of our Lord... and our faith in each other true and straight."

"Amen!" came the raised voices of the congregants, everyone thinking she was talking about the preacher who had disappeared. The man who had opened Pandora's box and the people who had not only been misled by him but attacked their good Reverend's reputation and that cost an innocent boy his life.

"We have stood up and accepted the challenge and used love and kindness and guts and courage to overcome the inequities flung at us. We have risen above the hatred, the jealousy, the greed and revenge seekers to bring forth a stronger belief in our faith and in ourselves." Matie's voiced penetrated the very fiber of the congregants, as she said these words straight at Dell Powell.

"AMEN!!" came the resounding chorus of voices from the congregation. But there was a sense that something was not right. Like an invisible wave passing through the congregation. They were missing something. But that thought slipped away.

And with that the Reverend Dr. Matie Cooper, hands holding the sides of the pulpit, raised her voice in joyous acclamation as the congregation rose to their feet with one glorious Halleluiah!

Before the first notes reverberated from the choir, Del Powell, who was sitting in his special reserved pew, stood up and moved into the aisle.

The stunned congregation went stone silent.

"You get down from my pulpit. You are a whore and a blasphemer. Women must bend to man's will! Not preach god's words! You have contaminated my church with your filth and fornication."

Del Powell ranted on and on as he kept walking towards the steps heading towards the Reverend. It looked like he was prepared to physically attack her.

Amel'iya made a move closer to the steps.

Old man Powell kept up his hate riddled tirade going red to purple as his eyes started to bulge.

From the audience a man could be heard, 'You tell her Del. She don't belong up there.' "

From another man came, "No woman belongs there preaching at us men." "

Then a third and a fourth voice could be heard. Their words of hate bouncing off the walls around the congregation.

Del Powell stopped a few feet from the steps and turned. Matie was standing behind the pulpit, staring straight at him. He began his tirade again, then stopped abruptly, stood still as stone and then fell face down on the floor, like a heavy felled tree.

The congregation gasped. Jacquelynn and Nathanial who were both already out of their seats, ran to the old man. Matie held her ground and called out, "Is there a doctor here? Is there a doctor here?

A half dozen men rose. The one nearest the fallen man rushed to his side.

He turned Powell over, took one looked at the face of a fatal irrevocable heart attack victim, and in conjunction with another physician pronounced Del Powell dead on the spot.

The paramedics were there in minutes and did try to revive him, but to no avail. The man was dead. Gone. Gone to his maker.

As the stunned congregation took their seats he was carted off. Matie Cooper was still standing at her pulpit. Jacqulyn looked towards her friend and Matie made the gesture for her to go with Nathanial. Jacqulyn nodded her head and followed the corpse with her husband.

"He dropped dead?" Mia exclaimed, very loudly.

"Dead as stone. Plus, by now the congregation knew that the Reverend had been talking at Dell Powell. The congregation, forgot entirely about the vanished preacher man.

"A wave of whispered uproar ran around the church as the skimpy facts and conjectures about Dell Powell were being embellished while the guesses rampaged around the congregations.

"From her place, at the pulpit, the Reverend Dr. Matie Cooper called for silence, "Please bend your head to pray for the soul of our recently departed ... "the Reverend Dr. Matie Cooper stopped abruptly.

"Br'Linda who are you sitting on?" The Reverend called out. Loud and clear. You should have seen it Mia. The whole congregation turned around like they had one head, looking for Br'Linda.

Br'Linda yelled back, "This here's a man I don't know, but what comes out of his mouth is disgusting blaspheming I do swear."

"Br'Linda would you please allow the good folk around you to help lift you off that lost-sheep?"

"Br'Linda looked at the man turning shades of red and then at the Reverend and noticed that it was quiet all around her. She lifted her arms and two sturdy friends helped her up.

"The man, trying to take a deep breath was lifted, taken to the back and put on a seat someone brought from the closet. He tried to get up to leave, but a large hand from behind pressed down on his shoulder, so he sat and fumed.

"Some of the men who had been encouraging Del had scampered off as soon as the call for a doctor was heard reverberating around the rafters. The other hecklers had taken their seats after being stared down by those they came with.

"Matie took a deep breath and lowered her head. They were going to say a prayer for the soul of the man; regardless of the hatred that spilt from his lips.

The congregation followed their Reverend. After which, choir, congregants, Deacons and Reverend raised their voice in a song of redemption and forgiveness.

It is said the sounds coming from the Springrock Baptist Church, that bright crisp Sunday morning, could be heard for miles around.

68

Mia was staring with eyes ready to pop out of her head, and speechless.

"I'll skip over all the church stuff and fuss that went on after that and jump ahead a bit."

"OK?"

Mia made just a little nod in affirmation. She might have been in overload.

I gave her my most assuring smile and continued, "As for Susan and your mom? They hustled back to college to be in time for your mom's latest race and Amel'iya and I stayed to tie up the loose ends in Gening.

"We helped get Matie settled in a rental with a great deal of help from her friends and congregants. Anything that could be salvaged from her house was put into storage.

"Amel'iya met her deadline by the way. She must have a time turning machine where she can do two or more things at once.

"As for me? I would have to restart what I was working on, but that was no big deal. It was the classes I was missing that were the problem. More sleepless nights were in front of me when I returned to school."

"There was no big fancy funeral service for Nathanial's father at Springrock, at the funeral home or at the grave. It appeared that when old man Powell died his large contributions to the church died with him.

"A simple burial was arranged, attended by the family and the Reverend Dr. Matie Cooper, who stood alongside Jacquelynn, Nathanial and their children plus friends who came there to support them.

"When the dust died down the young Powells were gone."

"They'd moved?"

I nodded my head.

"I guess I can understand that."

(Even after the first flash of gossip reached a crescendo, then petered out, there were still the stares, the room falling silent when one of them entered and the backs turned away. The shaming and aftermath, that everyone was feeling, about the enormity of two of their own race being thieves, one from their low ranks and one from their highest ranks, became too much for the younger Powells, especially the kids. They moved to Virginia, to a farm no less, a half hour out of D.C. and within driving distance from Matie's new congregation in the center of the state of Delaware.)

Yes Matie moved too. Chantal (one of Matie's good friends) had a cousin who she invited up to hear Reverend Dr. Matie Cooper. The reverend was still preaching and doing bible studies a month after the funeral. Her cousin was scouting around for a particular reverend for their struggling church.

Matie not only found one door closing but now another one was opening, To her amazement, the new door was a golden opportunity. They needed somene to build a church practically from scratch. A church that had an enthusiastic congregation that was looking for the "kindness" type of leader to preach and be a community organizer.

"So, did you find the shitfucker yet?" I asked David.

"Josiah Fortis's in the wind.

"I thought you'd be gone by now."

"Leaving in the morning. Casey and Susan are on the road."

"Any news that I don't know?"

"The police here tell me that his car's disappeared."

"It showed up at the airport in Albany. And no, he didn't get on a plane. And yes, I'm sure."

"I'll send you what I'm working on when it's 'smoothed'. It'll help with the next idiot who tries to do an identity theft stunt like Fortis tried."

"Looking forward to it, but you know it'll be obsolete in a week."

"Maybe six months, possibly a year I think. This one's on me for your help."

"Good. You're not in the budget here. Yet. (That was a hint. I didn't bite.) That will keep the firewalls up for a while."

"I think we'll need more than firewalls soon." I said.

"Sad to say I think you're right. Take care Claire Elizabeth. And remember you always have a job here."

He hung up before I could tell him where he could put his job offer.

"O.K. but what was the string my mom found? Matie asked.

"That would take us back to evening before Powell dropped dead.

"Let's see ..., there was you mom doing her best to make it as easy on your great-aunt as she could."

"Back to this Fortis guy." Casey said as every eye in the snug little vestry was fixated on her. It was so quiet that you couldn't hear a soul breathing.

"It all came down to a simple tax refund which I rode into digital theft and then blackmail The string was actually a simple stupid tax refund by a greedy man." At this Casey just smiled knowing that she had cracked the case and was kind of enjoying showing off.

Matie did that clear your voice thing to let her niece know that she should get on with it and stop the bragging before it became intolerable.

Casey moved her eyes to the left to see her aunt giving her the get on with it look and then continued, "Fortis was smart. I give him that. He played the con perfectly. And I wouldn't have caught him if he hadn't tried to squeeze out that tax refund. But he did. And that's how I caught him."

"We're losing you Casey."

"It was a little breadcrumb, I'll grant you. But I'm good at following bread crumbs. That's what a forensic accountant does. Which is part of the service I'm going to provide, by the way, when I open my own practice.

"Matie made a get on with the telling thing that she did before.

"Your mom got back on track as quick as she could, "So there was this bread crumb, a tax refund tucked inside all the stuff I'd found for her.

"The tax refund was sent to the preacher here in Gening from his last place. Issued electronically."

"That's a hint." I said to Mia whose eyes couldn't have gotten any wider than they were already.

"He used a false name but it was sent to Charmeur. I followed it," Casey continued, "and found some ident, gave it to Claire who found the preacher attached to Mr. Dell Powell by a long spider web route.

"I have to say, Claire Elizabeth, You and your contacts are magic."

Before Matie could do that thing with her voice Casey told us, "Anyway, Claire and I went back and forth for a while. There were a few doors that we had to be creative in opening. But before you start worrying Aunt Matie, we had the unofficial official blessing of the door keepers."

"Doorkeepers? Spider web? Casey! What are you talking about?" the Reverend Dr. Matie Cooper snapped.

"The FBI, the IRS, the agency we can't speak of, and of course that special get-of-jail card that my good friend here has." Casey said as she tossed a look my way. I cringed and swore I'd get even with her before the end of the day. (MY short but intense help at the request of the President of the United States had some benefits. Like making a call and having the person you want answer it. But it involved secrecy; like the, I'll have to kill you if I tell you, type of secrecy.)

"You're kidding! That's like the whole government!" Everyone in the room said to Casey, almost in unison.

"Not kidding one little bit. This identity theft thing is blowing up into a massive hurricane and a lot of people are looking to stop it or just figure out why it's so easy to do.

"Fortis's a crook, and he shouldn't get any accolades for being really smart but there's something to be said for anyone who could almost pull off what he did. If we weren't in his wake he might have gotten away with it again." Casey said as she rolled her eyes and tilted her head towards me again. "And when the tech gets better, and it will, it will be even harder to catch these kinds of bad guys."

"Will this Fortis man ever be caught?" Matie asked.

"He's disappeared into the wind; must have had an escape plane in place, but he'll surface somewhere; and there are a lot of people watching and waiting," Casey answered her aunt.

"Holy Shit!" Mia exclaimed.

"That expression is rather appropriate in the circumstances." I kidded.

"And mom figured this out and saved the Reverend?" Mia said seeing her mom in a new light. That is any other light other than the woman who birthed her, feeds her, houses her and makes her do her homework.

"You mom is one of the smartest women I know. And as determined as a hound dog after a scent. She never gives up and she will never turn her back on her friends or her family."

"Yeah," Mia said with a mischievous smile on her face, "and she will shoot a guy to save your life."

"Where in hell's name did you hear that load of crap?"

"Oh, just a little bird whispered in my ear."

"Well that little bird doesn't know what the hell he's talking about!"

"Right." Mia declared giving me a sideward look that said I was full of crap.

"Mia! Grace's brother saved my ass. End of story."

She hesitated for a moment not knowing whether to believe me or not. I hoped that she would come down on the side of ignorance. (And yes, Casey shot a guy who was about to kill me, but that is another story.)

Then, like all teenagers her attention went sideways. "I didn't know about my grandmother wanting to name my mom Case." After a moment's thought she asked, "Did the nurse get into trouble for putting the 'y' in?"

"Have no idea. But I wouldn't think so. I do know your mom was happy to change her last name to Buckhauser when she married your dad."

"Hey, do you know my dad and I asked Sam's husband, you know the one that's a Family Tree Zealot … ?"

"Zealot?"

"Well, he's got that whole thing going in his basement with trees and hundreds of names all over the walls – and he even has a program he told us you created for him to keep track of everything he finds out about black ancestry here in Gening. It's actually rather awesome.

"Anyway Mr. Robinson told us that he found out that our name came from a slave named Buck.

"He found out from the slave records that Buck was a house slave. It seems that the man who bought him was married to a German lady who called my ancestor Buck Haus (for house). Somewhere along the line Buck Haus turned into Buck Hauser; sometimes just plain Hauser. Then he was sold.

"Mr. Robinson told us that when Buck was sold his name was registered as Buckhauser. I guess it could have been worse. His name might have been turned into Buckimhaus or Buck Imhaus or Buck Imhauser.

"I never heard that story."

"My mom told me that she hated having her dad's name tagged onto her. He father was kind of a shit abuser.

"Never met the guy. None of our homes were places where we'd want to bring anyone to. Our lives happened in school and on our teams."

"That is so sad."

"Lots of stuff is sad."

"Sorry, did I make you remember your bad stuff?"

"Just around the edges. Now," I said as I stood up, "off you go."

69

Back in Gening, before we all scattered to our normal lives, Amel'iya told Matie, "I checked on Stellie's brother. He is indeed where his sister said he is. Also found out that he's real happy where he's at. Has a family, a great job and between you and me I don't think he'll ever invite his sister to come live with him.

"As for Nikki, I don't think she's given up yet. You need to keep an eye out for her."

"But why did she do that?" Matie asked.

"Jealousy would be my bet. She probably thought she'd be high up on the ladder if her fiancé was the reverend here. And you squashed that dream. "

"And jealousy can turn to wrath." Matie countered.

"Wrath?" I asked not being up on all the religious stuff.

"Hate." Matie interpreted.

"There's a lot of that around here Reverend. There's a lot of men in this town who don't like women preaching to them. They're an ugly bunch.

But then there are a lot who don't much mind. Maybe it will all balance itself out." Matie thought out loud. "But I still don't understand why that Josiah Fortis person chose me"

"It was Dell Powell he chose. Then he looked for someone to take the blame after he cleaned out Powell's accounts. And there were a lot of accounts as it turned out.'

"You mean I was just a … a SUPERNUMERARY? That's …. that's …. I don't know what that is, but it makes me feel like I'm invisible, just a pawn or something."

"Don't feel bad Reverend. He'd done it before and gotten away with it. But we stopped him. Keep remembering, it was Casey who found the proverbial essential string. We pulled and pulled on it, and Josiah Fortis is now in the wind and no threat to you or any of us."

"But that's when my great aunt left Gening? Wasn't it?" Mia said, "so maybe there still was a threat? Or was she asked to leave or fired?" Mia asked, kind of not wanting to hear this part.

"It seems that when one door slams shut another one opens my little one. And that seems to be what happened to your great-aunt; because a better opportunity came along. Better for her anyway."

"She really likes her congregation and the people down there in Delaware."

"As I said one door closes and another opens up. You just have to be able to see the opportunity."

"O.K. I've got to get back. And thanks godmother." Mia leaned over, kissed me goodbye, ran out and silence gently drifted over my space.

Heaven.

70

(The final report on the death of Malcolm took months before it made its way into the official light of day. It didn't identify the person responsible for Malcolm Farley's death.)

But Amel'iya came up with the best scenario to fit the facts. It hit all the points, dead on, so to speak.

Her version: The non-descript tan van slowly pulled into the church's back lot. It didn't make any lasting impression on the church greeter who was busy opening up the front door at that time. The person with a cap pulled down low hiding the driver's face therefore didn't make any impression on his memory either.

She was smart about that van, Amel'iya said. So many places filled with old worn out vehicles all over New York. Places that take cash and ask no questions. In fact she probably chose a business known to leave the keys in the car's well. These places let you ride off with the vehicle you want, with no guarantee that it would work, but usually they do, and when you return it, you leave money in the side pocket of the door under the seat. I'll bet her husband used vehicles from this business years ago and the old man, there's always an old man, was still there.

I'm guessing, but I'll bet the greasy overblown owner wasn't there when she took the van. He won't be about to answer any questions if the cops come around; and he'd not be the sort to offer any unsolicited information even if he knew something.

But she was smart. If there had been a working camera outside the lot, it wouldn't show her face. She'd be covered up. And she would return that wreck and walk away to some garage nearby where she'd get her own car.

This was about as good as untraceable as it could get, to my way of thinking.

Our response: "SHE??" We all yelled.

"Michelle Goodman." Amel'iya said matter-of-factly.

"But they couldn't pin it on her!" Casey exclaimed as we all looked on. (We, being all eight of us who were on shore leave, school leave or had just stopped what we were doing in order to gather as was our custom.)

(Yes! We all think Amel'iya might be from another galaxy, but she has this sixth sense, that is … well … that is unusual. Let's leave it at that.)

Amel'iya wasn't that far off the mark as we found out months later when Detective Michaels turned in his report.

Susan, our cross the t's and dot the i's leader, took all the pieces and put the script together. (She'd have made a superb prosecutor, but she went for what she wanted; a husband who was a Judge.)

Susan's version: Michelle had driven into the church lot with some of the earlier arrivers. She'd chosen a spot hidden mostly by the back edge of the church. A spot close enough to the delivery entrance to make it look like it was there for a purpose. Then she hunkered down, out of sight.

Her plan was to wait, hidden in the van, until the last car filled the lot.

Then she had to wait for the music and singing to start.

My heart was sure racing. She thought. But it was easy. I rolled the car close to that side wall, pulled the van door open and dumped his dead weight against the wall. I bet it took all of two minutes and then I was headed out of town. Easy.

She'd returned home, after returning the van to one of those no-tell wreck of a car places, in time to see the tail end of the chaos at the church. She heard the accusations and lies flying about.

It was like watching a beehive gone berserk. Michelle Goodman must have thought.

The chatter continued that evening and well into the next day.

Her phone didn't stop ringing.

She laughed out loud. The boy's father accusing Matie Cooper of killing his son was fucking perfect.

She would get her revenge. And they wouldn't catch her. And the Cooper woman would be gone.

It was divine providence. That's what it was. Passing the boy like that the other day. When I stopped him and asked him if he could use a hundred to help me with some digging holes for some new bushes and cleaning up the yard he said sure. The silly boy didn't suspect anything.

She hadn't noticed that he looked clean and clear eyed when he showed up very early Sunday morning. She mistook a sleepy teenager for a drug user.

She'd tell herself - he was probably good at hiding his use. Sure, I hadn't seen him for months but a drug addict is always a drug addict.

He'd opened the side door of the van to get the tools out, he thought. But she clamped a high dose of chloroform over his face. He struggled a little, but she was a strong woman.

Her husband had left a lot of stuff around the house, like the chloroform and other paraphernalia. Years before, when she'd asked him why he had all this stuff he'd turned on her telling her to mind her own fuckin business.

She didn't like to think about that time. His anger and the way he looked at her.

She brushed that memory away as she stood at her window.

Michelle Goodman kept watching as the street cleared out.

Earlier there had been an officer who came by to ask her if she had seen anything unusual. But having him at her front door only gave her a momentary spike of fear.

What Michelle Goodman didn't know, because she couldn't see what was going on behind the church from her widow, was that Susan and then Detective Michaels had walked the lot winding up at an empty spot behind the church.

He did a three sixty and came to the conclusion that this was probably the best spot to park if you wanted to be practically unnoticed.

Then it was time to interview all the practitioners who had parked within view of the empty space.

When the Reverend and Casey came in the next morning, the police knew that there had been an old tan van in the lot before the services began. Of course, they knew that Matie Cooper had never left the church after she arrived around six that morning, having been seen walking from her house to the church; and there were a load of witnesses to verify that fact; but Matie was still devastated that she was suspected. Someone hated her enough to take the life of a troubled young man in order to do her irreputable harm.)

Detective Michaels went back to re-interview Ms. Goodman. He wanted to know where she was up until her neighbor saw her car return at eleven fifteen.

"I went for a walk on the rail-trail. My doctor says I need more exercise."

"Did anyone see you?" the Detective asked.

"Of course people saw me." The briefest of panic in her eyes turned dark into belligerence.

"Anyone who can verify you were walking on the trail?" the detective said in an even firm tone.

"How would I know?"

"If it was someone who knew you, you would have probably said hello to them."

"Well I didn't see anyone I know." She said crossing her arms tightly across her chest.

After a difficult discussion with his chief, a warrant was issued and another hefty chunk of Chief Wojcik's budget went into vacuuming and examining every scrape of dirt and piece of detritus found in her house and garage.

What they found was that every inch was too neat, too organized, too clean, too scrubbed, too soaked in Clorox and no dust was found on, in or around the garage wall with cabinets that could hide contraband.

The shelves, cabinets and even the studs were spotless.

Wood samples were taken.

The findings on the efforts to place the old drugs used to kill Malcolm Farley in or near her home were inconclusive.

And when Michelle Goodman was questioned about her husband's association with the men from old matching drug cases, she insisted that her husband never had anything to do with those people, all who wound up in jail or dead.

So ... everything was all circumstantial.

Michelle Goodman had a reason, opportunity and means. But, the prosecutor said there wasn't enough concrete evidence to take to court. So ... case Closed.)

71

Two weeks later, after retelling the Preacher-Story to Mia, someone was banging on my front door, loudly - and ringing the bell at the same time.

It was a feeling like a déjà vu moment.

I looked over to my outside six box screen to see Mia looking up into the security camera (still banging on the door and still ringing the bell).

I sighed and crossed the room to let her in. As soon as the door was open Mia came barging in saying, rather loudly, "Claire you have to get dressed and come over to my house, like right now."

I looked at her, hard, waiting, for about half a millisecond until she responded. "Susan's over there and she and mom are going to call a meeting of Class '94.

"What's the emergency!" I asked, as my heart beat rose a few octaves.

"Well it's not an emergency, maybe ... but maybe it is ... I don't know. Get dressed."

She actually grabbed my sleeve and started pulling me towards the steps to my closet upstairs; where she arrived four steps in front of me and proceeded to go through my closet, coming out less than a minute later, with an outfit. And shoes. And a belt.

"You're as bad as Grace."

"No I'm not, she can do it faster."

So I got dragged over to Casey's house where the door was opened as soon as my foot hit the front step. At the second step Susan reached out and grabbed me, pulling me inside

"Stop all the grabby hand thing," I barked, pushing her hand away.

As soon as Susan got me into the living room, pushing me now, she took the printouts Casey was holding out for her and pushed them in front of my face.

I took them.

There in front of me, on top of the printouts, was a full frontal view of the long lost Preacher Charmer AKA Josiah Fort.

The next page and the pages afterwards contained all sorts of personal information. From driver's license (new name) address, phone numbers, of which there were a few, home address, a deed, a blueprint of said home, and to top it off - information about his bank accounts from numbers to amounts to whereabouts.

By this time my mouth have fallen open, the room was filled with all seven of us – plus Mia and Matie - and I was somewhere between shock and double shock.

I looked up to see nine pairs of eyes looking back at me

I said, "It can't be. It can't be him. It just can't be! HOW!"

"The program you set up, to alert us if or when his image or name came up anywhere."

"But that was ... almost twenty years ago! It's not working anymore. I never updated it."

"Well it obviously IS still working." Casey said.

I looked at all of them shaking my head back and forth. "No. It's not working."

They looked at me.

Mia and Matie were looking all around the room not knowing whom to rest their eyes on.

"No! It's not her!" I emphatically stated.

Susan shrugged her shoulder. Whitney's eyes opened wide. Sam gave Grace a nasty look and Grace just Cheshire smiled back at Sam.

Char'Elene didn't hear the penny drop. Casey draped her arm around her confused friend and whispered in her ear.

Char'Elene's eyes popped, after the penny dropped, and she yelled, "NO! It can't be."

Afterwords

After Mia left with a few blanks in her history now filled in, I started swiveling back and forth in my chair staring out into my walled garden.

Then I realized I'd never asked her why her great aunt was coming for such an extended stay.

Whatever.

Two months later, Matie was still here and I realized I still hadn't asked.

Stuff goes flying out of my head these days with so much going on around me.

Also, I'd been so busy that I rarely got to visit with Matie while she was here. So I never found out why she came in the first place, is what I'm trying to say. (I know, it's a lame excuse.)

Then Casey called a meet.

Before I get to that.

Let's go back a few lines.

Yes, in the end, it was Amel'iya who'd found the scumfortis . Like who else could or would it have been?

We all agreed.

We agreed to feed him to the alphabet agency in Washington D.C. who are meaner than we could ever be.

So! Amel'iya was back in our lives.

Long story short, I'm not happy - but Fortis is behind bars.

That was a few years ago.

Amel'iya's been back for about two years, and then the shit hit the fan. Really bad shit.

Some white nationalist cretins decided to murder Susan's husband. He's a federal judge, so you can just imagine the fireworks that set off.

Amel'iya almost got there in time to stop the killers. Lots of shooting, some dead white shitholes, lots of FBI, police and panic.

The judge and Susan were shot.

It scared the shit out of all of us. Like scared into hyperventilating paralysis.

Susan recovered quickly, the judge not so fast. Military style weapons tear a human body apart.

And then there was the midnight moving of the judge before another attempt could be made on his life. It was something out of a mobster movie. A really bad B movie.

Amel'iya (who can't be scared shitless; I think) was literally given an FBI gun person to work the security.

She worked with Amel'iya after they got the judge out of intensive care and even afterwards. (O.K. I liked Amel'iya again by now – almost.)

The judge was hurt real bad. No one thinks he'll be able to preside over a court again

And Amel'iya? Well she has lots of guns, knives, nasty things she throws at the bad guys that explode and a big black government grade SUV. (And NO, we still don't know exactly what she does.)

But back to Casey calling a meet.

Matie was still here and Grace and Sam had just come back from their second store in New York. Whitney was painting but worrying over her kids. Char'Elene was aggressively fending off an outrageously lucrative offer to work someplace in the Arab world where men keep women covered, sequester and misused. My past associate David, who was now a big honcho at the CIA, was behind the scenes to make sure Char'Elene was safe.

And Casey calls a meet. Something more was going on. Something big. And I had no fuckin clue as to what it was.

The End